"It isn't safe out h
get back to the h

Jennie stared at the proffered hand for a moment before slipping hers into it. "I can't hide forever, Cameron. The ranch can't handle itself."

"You have three ranch hands, let them do it. They aren't the ones under the gun."

"No, but with all the accusations flying, one of them might be the one holding that gun."

"All the more reason for you to stay in the house." Cameron moved along the base of the tree line toward the house, alert. Too often today, he'd let himself be distracted. He couldn't afford it. Perhaps his boss was right and he was too close to Jennie to be proper protection for her.

But then he turned and looked at her and realized that the thought of relinquishing the task to someone else was not an option he'd even consider.

ELLE JAMES

COWBOY SANCTUARY

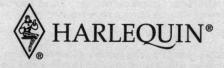

TORONTO • NEW YORK • LONDON
AMSTERDAM • PARIS • SYDNEY • HAMBURG
STOCKHOLM • ATHENS • TOKYO • MILAN • MADRID
PRAGUE • WARSAW • BUDAPEST • AUCKLAND

This book is dedicated to my fellow authors in the BODYGUARDS UNLIMITED, DENVER, CO series who helped provide inspiration and the glue to stick this project together. And to the amazing editors, Sean Mackiewicz and Allison Lyons, who dreamed up the story line and who invited me to be a part of the project, thank you.

Special thanks and acknowledgment are given to Elle James for her contribution to the BODYGUARDS UNLIMITED, DENVER, CO miniseries.

ISBN-13: 978-0-373-69254-5
ISBN-10: 0-373-69254-4

COWBOY SANCTUARY

ABOUT THE AUTHOR

Elle was a 2004 Golden Heart Winner for Best Paranormal Romance; she started writing when her sister issued the Y2K challenge to write a romance novel. She managed a full-time job, raised three wonderful children, and she and her husband even tried their hands at ranching exotic birds—ostriches, emus and rheas—in the Texas hill country. Ask her, and she'll tell you what it's like to go toe-to-toe with an angry 350-pound bird! After leaving her successful career in information technology management, Elle is now pursuing her writing full-time. She loves building exciting stories about heroes, heroines, romance and passion. Elle loves to hear from fans. You can contact her at ellejames@earthlink.net or visit her Web site at www.ellejames.com

Books by Elle James

HARLEQUIN INTRIGUE

CAST OF CHARACTERS

Cameron Morgan—The black sheep of the Morgan family and bodyguard for Prescott Personal Securities returns to his home to convince his family and their feuding neighbors they are in danger.

Jennie Ward—Once in love with Cameron despite their two families' differences, she refused to leave her father and the ranch when Cameron left ten years ago. How can she protect her heart from the danger of falling in love again?

Evangeline Prescott—The owner of Prescott Personal Securities who assigns Cameron to help the ranch owners.

Tom Morgan—Owner of the Bar M Ranch and Cameron's stubborn father. Will he ever forgive his son for loving the enemy's daughter?

Logan Morgan—Cameron's moody brother. Why is he still so angry at Cameron?

Brad Carter—Hired hand on the Morgan ranch. Is he there to only help himself?

Hank Ward—Owner of the Flying W and Jennie's father. Will the attempts on his life leave Jennie to run the ranch on her own?

Vance Franklin—Jennie's husband who died eight years ago.

Doug Sweeney—Hank Ward's longtime ranch hand.

Stan Keller—The Flying W ranch foreman and Hank Ward's old friend.

Rudy Toler—The youngest ranch hand on the Flying W.

Prologue

Jennie Ward fought to stay in the saddle as Lady bucked beneath her like a green filly on her first ride. What was wrong with her? The eight-year-old mare hadn't behaved like this since she saw that six-foot diamond-back rattlesnake two years ago.

No matter how accomplished a rider, Jennie knew she wouldn't last long at the rate Lady was jerking her around. She had to get off or be thrown off.

Clutching the saddle horn for balance, she decided that on the count of three, she'd jump. One…two… Jennie kicked her feet free of the stirrups…three! As Lady hit the ground in a bone-jarring, stiff-legged bounce, Jennie shoved against the saddle, launching herself into the air and as far away from the frantic horse as she could manage.

She landed on her hands and knees, rocks gouging her kneecaps, tearing through her denim jeans. Her head banged against the ground, and her vision blurred for a split second. She couldn't pass out. Not here. Not with a thousand-pound quarter horse thrashing around her. She tucked her arms and legs close to her body and rolled to the side to avoid the horse's hooves. As soon as she was clear, she scrambled to her feet and scurried behind a tree.

Lady tossed around for another minute before she halted in the middle of the field, flanks lathered and quivering.

When Jennie approached, the horse's eyes rolled and she backed away, whinnying a warning.

Jennie cast a quick glance around at the ground. She couldn't see a snake, varmint or anything resembling one. "What's wrong with you, girl?" She eased forward, speaking in a soft crooning voice, holding her hand out for the mare to sniff. When she stood close enough, she snagged the reins and patted the mare's neck. "It's okay. Shhhhh. I won't hurt you, baby."

The dusky black mare danced in a semicircle straining against the hold Jennie had on the reins. After the horse quieted, Jennie eased alongside her and ran her hand down the horse's legs, searching for signs of injury.

The horse's legs appeared to be fine. When Jennie bent to lift the back left leg to examine Lady's hoof, something warm and wet dripped across her temple. Reaching up, she brushed the moisture from her face with her hand. She glanced down at her fingers where bright red liquid stood out against the light gray of her work gloves.

Blood? Had she cut her head when she fell? She yanked the gloves from her hands, reached up to where she'd hit her head and found a small lump the size of a quarter against her hairline. When she brought her hand down, there was no blood.

Then she looked at the horse. Blood soaked the multicolored saddle blanket and dripped to the ground below. "Holy smokes, Lady. What the hell happened?"

Jennie led the horse to the nearest tree, tied her up, giving her very little slack from her head to the tree. Skimming her fingers along the horse's neck, she worked her hands over to the saddle, the source of the horse's obvious pain.

What was causing the bleeding? Lady had been fine when she'd saddled up less than fifteen minutes earlier.

She laid the stirrup gently over the top of the saddle, talking to the horse the entire time. With one hand she loosened the cinch strap and pulled it free. Using as much care as she could muster, Jennie eased the saddle from the horse's back, lifting it straight up and off. Lady leaned hard against the reins, swinging her backside away from Jennie and the saddle.

The sheepskin lining on the underside of the saddle was soaked in blood as was the blanket still on the horse's back.

When Jennie lifted the blanket, Lady whimpered, her ears laid back and her withers twitched. Jutting out of the middle of a bloody patch was the metal corner of a razor blade.

"Oh my God." No wonder Lady tried to throw her. The entire time she'd been riding, the razor dug deeper into the horse's flesh. Lady's back was clean when she'd tossed the blanket over her in the barn.

Jennie raised the blanket and found a cut in the middle where the razor had sliced through. An inspection of the saddle revealed another cut buried in the sheepskin underside.

They didn't use razor blades in the barn and none of the ranch hands shaved anywhere near the horses.

Then how the hell did the blade end up in her saddle?

Leaving the saddle and blanket on the ground, Jennie

untied Lady and led her back toward the barn. She'd return later for the saddle and blanket. First, she needed to tend to her horse's injury, and then she'd find out what happened.

As she walked, she pondered the conundrum of the razor blade. They had no reason to store razor blades in the tack room. How could it have gotten in there and under her saddle? The saddle normally rested on a saddletree inside the tack room. A razor blade would have fallen off. Could someone have intentionally planted the razor in her saddle? The idea made her sick to her stomach. Who would be so cruel to a horse? Another thought followed close behind the first. Had someone intended to hurt her?

If so, why? There had to be a logical explanation. Who would want to hurt her? She didn't have any enemies except the Morgans and they stayed on their ranch. For the past ten years, not a single Morgan dared cross the boundaries between the Flying W and the Bar M. The only person who'd ever wanted to hurt her was her ex-husband, and he was dead.

Chapter One

Cameron Morgan pulled his cowboy hat from his head, leaned his eye against the scanner next to the door and waited for the green light to pan across his eyeball. When the lock clicked open, he straightened and stepped through the heavy glass doors into the spacious offices of Prescott Personal Securities. After being gone for the past month on assignment, he felt as if he was coming home. He inhaled, expecting the soothing scents of eucalyptus and furniture polish. Instead, an acrid aroma stung his nostrils.

"Hi, Angel," he said to the receptionist behind the bleached pine countertop. Cameron wrinkled his nose. "Was there a chemical spill somewhere?"

Angel, the street punk adopted by the agency's owner out of some attempt at being charitable, rolled her eyes. "'Sup?" She barely looked up as she smacked her gum between black lipstick-covered lips while she painted another coat of dead black polish on her clawlike fingernails.

Cameron wrinkled his nose. Ah, the source of the odor. "Do you have to do that here?"

She answered by raising her brows. No wonder

memos from Angel were often misspelled and calls were misdirected. With nails like that, she couldn't possibly hit the right keys on the computer keyboard or the telephone switchboard. Despite the everything-black, Goth look, she showed an occasional spark of intelligence that invariably took everyone by surprise and she was puppy-dog loyal to the boss.

"Any messages?" he asked.

"Give me a few, and I'll check." She capped the fingernail polish and shook her hands, blowing on the wet paint.

"A few" meant some time in the next hour or two—*if* she remembered after the paint fumes subsided and her brain activity reengaged.

Cameron shook his head and continued on to his office.

Before he'd gone five steps, Angel called out, "Hey, wait. I was supposed to tell you something."

Perhaps the cloud of vapor had cleared and she was remembering. Cameron turned and smiled, encouraging the young woman.

Her pale forehead wrinkled and her thickly lined eyes squinted to slits. "Oh, yeah, the boss wants you in the conference room."

"When?" Cameron tapped his Stetson against his thigh.

She stopped chewing her gum long enough to snort and say, "Like, now. I believe her words were ASAP." She resumed blowing on her nails and smacking her gum.

Letters. A S A and P are letters. Cameron inhaled and blew out a calming stream of air before he smiled again. This wasn't the first time Angel had delayed an urgent message or misdirected a memo. He couldn't even count the number of times they'd had to call the repairman to fix the copier after she'd done whatever she did to break it. One of the machine mechanics had gone so far as to nickname her the Angel of Death. "Thanks, Angel. What would we all do without you?" *Hire a real secretary?*

"I don't know, but you better hurry," she said without looking up.

When Cameron entered the conference room, every gaze turned toward him. Four other agents sat around the table and an elegant blonde stood at the head. He nodded toward his friend, Jack Sanders, seated to his left and then fixed his attention on the woman standing, Evangeline Prescott, head of Prescott Personal Securities. "You wanted to see me?"

With her long blond hair pulled back in a French twist and wearing a medium gray skirt suit, Evangeline was a cool professional with a warm smile. She looked much better than she had when she'd first lost her husband in a plane crash two years ago. Perhaps she was finally moving on.

Evangeline stood with a laser pointer resting in her palm and her back turned to a projected view of a map depicting the state of Colorado. With a brief smile she nodded toward a seat. "Good. You got my message. If you'll take a seat, I'll explain why you're here." She nodded, the few curls that had managed to escape bobbed with the motion. "Remember the disk that arrived at the office during the Nick Warner case?"

The head of Prescott Personal Securities made it a point to keep all bodyguards abreast of the caseload. Cameron nodded.

"Cassie deciphered the codes and she's been working with Lenny to figure out what exactly we have and what it means."

"How's that going?" Cameron glanced from Cassie, who hadn't looked up yet, to William Lennard, affectionately nicknamed Lenny, the group's incredibly adept techno geek.

"Good, Cam, real good." The red-haired young man's gaze remained affixed to the computer screen. He clicked the keys and the image on the big screen zoomed closer.

Cameron was used to Lenny being less than communicative at times. When he got wrapped up in solving a computer puzzle, he lost track of everything else, including time and polite conversation. Which made the hairs on the back of Cameron's neck rise. What was Lenny working on now?

Cameron's gaze panned to Mike Lawson and Cassie Allen sitting close together, peering at a printout on the table between them. Mike glanced up and nodded. "We've made a little progress." He nudged Cassie, who looked to Mike first. Deaf since college, she hadn't heard Cameron enter. When she turned toward him, her face lit with a smile. "Hi, Cameron."

He nodded and remained standing. "So what did you find on the disk?" *And what does it have to do with me?*

"Actually, we think the disk is full of land coordinates. Lenny was just showing us where one of those coordinates is in the state of Colorado. Would you do us the honors?" Evangeline glanced at their techno geek.

Lenny clicked a single key. The projected view zoomed in until Cameron could read the town names— one in particular.

"Are you familiar with a small town northwest of Denver called Dry Wash?" Evangeline used the laser pointer to indicate the position on the map.

Was he familiar? Did spending the first eighteen years of your life count toward familiarity? Cameron molded the brim of the light brown Stetson in his hands. "Yes. It's my hometown." He directed his stare to Evangeline, his eyes narrowing. "But you know that."

Evangeline nodded. "The coordinates pinpoint a location near there. I had Lenny pull up the online county plats and overlay it with the exact coordinates."

Cameron stepped closer to the screen, recognition igniting the nerves in his gut. Lines drawn over an aerial photograph delineated the Bar M Ranch from the Flying W Ranch to the south. The point on the map indicated an area on the border between the two ranches. "The Bar M is my father's ranch and the Flying W belongs to Hank Ward." He glanced at Evangeline. "What's the significance of the location?"

"We don't know exactly, but we know a little more about some of the other coordinates." Evangeline nodded to Lenny. "Show him the other view, please."

"Yes, ma'am." Lenny clicked several keys and a broader view of Colorado appeared on the screen with red dots sprinkled across the map.

"These are some of the other coordinates listed on the disk." She pointed to two of them. "We've researched these two. The land is owned by a company called Tri Corp. Media." She shot a glance toward Mike. "Mike, tell them what you found out about these locations."

Mike's face was poker straight. "They're known to be rich in oil and…they were previously owned by

Milo Kardascian and James Durgin, our dead CEOs. They sold their companies and land for cash and shares in Kingston Trust to pay off debt."

"So you have two CEOs who sold out for cash and shares, Tri Corp. Media bought the companies and land and both CEOs are now dead." Cameron shrugged. "Sounds suspicious. Why don't you take it to the police?"

Jack shook his head. "And tell them what? We don't have any solid evidence to point toward Tri Corp. Media. For all we know TCM is just a company that knows when to make a good deal."

Evangeline paced in front of the screen, the light from the projector painting mottled images across her gray suit. "All we have is this land coordinate and the disk. That and a few other puzzle pieces."

"What puzzle pieces?"

Mike jumped in. "Durgin came to us scared he would be the next man murdered from a list of Kingston Trust investors."

None of this was making much sense to Cameron. "Why don't you go to the investment company that manages the trust and get the list of investors?"

"That's just it, it's a blind trust," Evangeline responded. "They don't have to share the names of the investors unless we get a court order and send in the police. We don't have enough evidence to do that yet. We're going on supposition."

Lenny raised his hand. "I'm checking into Kingston and hope to know something soon."

Mike added, "There's also Milo Kardascian's connection to the Russian mob through his gambling debts."

"Wait a minute. Do you think the Russian mob is

involved in this?" Cameron tapped his hat against his thigh, his brain scrambling to take it all in.

Evangeline's shoulders rose and fell. "We're not certain of anything yet. We do know Kardascian was a habitual gambler. He frequented the mob-run private gambling establishments in Central City where he gambled his way deep into debt."

Jack snorted. "And the mob demands payment in one form or another."

With too many questions and not enough answers, Cameron wasn't liking where this investigation was going. "Do you think the mob or the owners of the trust are going to go after this land because of the oil?"

"Possibly." Cassie had been watching Cameron intently, reading his lips. "Rather be safe than sorry. Apparently each investor only knows the name of one other investor as far as we can tell. We only know of the two who've died recently."

Evangeline picked up the story. "Durgin had been told he himself was a target by the investor who had his name. Durgin knew only one other name, but he didn't get to tell us before he was murdered. He was scared and asked for our protection. Unfortunately, someone got to him."

"Let me get this straight. A business deal is about to go down somewhere along the border of the Bar M and the Flying W."

Evangeline nodded. "That's what we think."

"Are we looking at a possible payment or a transfer of land or mineral rights?" Cameron asked.

Evangeline glanced at Rick and Cassie. "Apparently, the two CEOs sold their land before they knew it was rich in oil. They might not have known about the oil, but someone else did. Maybe the Russian mob that let

Milo rack up a huge gambling debt, or the owner of the Kingston Trust. Maybe TCM has a hand in this. We don't know yet. We do know that once the CEOs invested in the trust with their companies and land, they were murdered."

For several seconds, the news sank in. A knot formed in the pit of Cameron's belly. "You think that once they get the owners to sell or invest their land in the Kingston Trust, they kill them to keep the profits for themselves?"

"You tell me. We're just guessing at this point."

"What if the landowners don't want to sell?" Cameron asked. "I know these people, their families have ranched that land all their lives."

Mike tapped a pen to the table. "Kardascian and Durgin were forced to sell to get out of debt."

"These ranchers don't gamble." Cameron snorted. "Hell, they don't have time. They're too busy trying to eke out a living raising cattle."

"There are other ways to force people out." Evangeline stared hard at Cameron. "They could ruin the business so they're forced to sell. They've proven themselves ruthless, who's to say they won't take more drastic measures?"

Cameron froze. "You mean kill them and buy the property from the estate?"

"We don't know for sure, but maybe. It looks like the Dry Wash location is the next acquisition target. That's why we brought you in."

Lenny clicked a key and the view screen zoomed in on the county plat map. The Bar M and the Flying W property lines reappeared in clear, clean lines.

Cameron stood still, his heart pounding in his chest and his thoughts racing ahead to the Bar M Ranch, his father, mother, brother and sister. Were they in danger? Surely they wouldn't target an entire family to get the property. There were five of them, counting himself.

His gaze shifted to the Flying W, unless they planned to go after the low-hanging fruit. Hank Ward's wife, Louise, had died eighteen years ago. They'd only had one child.

Jennie.

The air left his lungs in a rush. Jennie Ward. His Jennie.

Only she wasn't his Jennie anymore. She'd married right after he left ten years ago. Although widowed now, she had no children of her own, that left just the two Wards—Hank and Jennie.

"What's the game plan?" Cameron's gaze swept the room coming to rest on Evangeline.

"We think the Wards and the Morgans need some warning about what might happen, and we recommend bodyguards."

Cameron snorted. "Neither one of the families will ever believe they need a bodyguard. They're ranchers. They take care of their own."

"I was thinking of sending Jack in to speak to them," Evangeline continued.

Already shaking his head, Cameron shot a look at Jack. "No offense, but they won't listen to an outsider. My father might listen, because he knows Jack. Hank Ward is an entirely different story."

"You know him?" Evangeline asked.

"Yes, ma'am." Cameron dropped his hand, running the brim of his Stetson through his fingers. "But he won't listen to a stranger."

"Then could you go with Jack to make sure they take the threat seriously?" Evangeline asked.

The air in the room pressed in around Cameron. Go to the Flying W? Would Jennie be there? Ten years was a long time. Why did he still feel such a strong tug in his chest when he thought of Jennie? "The Wards and the Morgans have been feuding for close to thirty years. Don't think it would do much good."

Evangeline's blue eyes darkened. "I don't care if the Hatfields and McCoys are feuding, someone has to tell these people what they're up agai—"

"I'll go." Cameron couldn't believe the words jumped out of his mouth. The more he thought about it, the more he realized Jennie could be in danger. Jack was an excellent agent, one of the best, and he'd do a good job. However, Cameron couldn't live with himself if something happened to Jennie and he wasn't there to stop it. "I'll go," he repeated.

Evangeline's mouth was still open from her last word. She shut it and tipped her head to the side. "You're the right man to inform your family, but maybe Jack should speak to the Wards."

"Look, I never went along with the feud. I thought it was a stupid waste of time." That had always been the problem in his father's eyes. If he'd stuck to the Morgan's side of the fence, he never would have fallen in love with Jennie and he and his family would still get along. "Let me speak to the Wards."

JENNIE SWUNG HER LEG over her mount and dropped to the hard-packed dirt. With Lady out of commission, she'd had to ride Little Joe and his gait wasn't as smooth as Lady's. Every muscle and joint ached from fourteen hours in the saddle. Thank goodness the temperatures had only been in the seventies.

She loved the spring. After the long months of winter with the wind howling through the valleys, she looked forward to the warmer days and clear blue skies. On the other hand, she dreaded the long hot days and dust of summer.

With the three-year drought and cattle prices down, they'd had to let the extra hands go. Which meant, along with Stan Keller, their foreman, and Rudy Toler and Doug Sweeney, the two remaining cowhands, Jennie rode fences and checked cattle every day. This year had to be better than last. They couldn't afford to keep the cattle and the ranch if they weren't making enough money to buy feed, much less pay the hands. So far the year had been one disaster after another.

Her father had always managed the books, but being shorthanded meant doing all the work themselves. Every able-bodied man and woman would be out tending stock and fences, except the housekeeper, Ms. Blainey. Her job was as important as tending cattle. She cooked the meals for the worn-out cowhands.

Her stomach rumbling, Jennie hurried to feed, brush and curry the bay gelding. After reapplying the dressing to Lady's injury, she made her way to the house intent on soaking in a hot shower before dinner. She still didn't have a clue where the razor blade had come from and none of the hands owned up to leaving it in the tack room. She'd warned them to inspect their gear before saddling up, just in case.

Her father should be back from checking on stock in the north pasture soon. He knew how upset Ms. Blainey would be if he missed supper. Jennie smiled. Rachel Blainey was the same age her mother would have been if she'd lived this long, and she was a nice addition to the staff. Jennie hated cooking with a passion. She'd rather wrestle an ornery bull-calf than bake a cake. Her smile slipped. She hoped they could keep Ms. Blainey on, as tight as the money was.

Vowing to stay awake long enough to review the accounts that night, Jennie trudged up past the bunkhouse. When the sprawling cedar-and-stone cabin came into view, she spied a strange, black four-wheel-drive pickup parked in the gravel driveway. Company? They weren't expecting any company, were they?

She frowned down at her filthy shirt and dusty jeans and sighed. Couldn't be helped. Whoever it was would just have to understand she'd been out working. Her mother would have rushed her back inside and made her take a shower before greeting guests. But that was when she was ten and her mother was always at the house, clean, pressed and looking like a model fresh from a magazine shoot, instead of a cattle rancher's wife.

After eighteen years, Jennie could still remember the smell of her mother's perfume and envision the smile, very much like her own. Sometimes she missed her mother more than she could bear—usually when times were toughest. But her father had done the best he could and loved her enough for both parents.

Jennie stepped in through the back door. She could hear the low rumble of a male voice coming from the living room and the happy sound of Ms. Blainey's laughter.

Maybe she did have time to shower and change before she came out. Easing her way down the hallway, she was almost to the staircase when a soft, feminine voice called out, "Hank? Is that you?" Rachel Blainey rounded the corner from the living room, her dark hair pulled back from her face, her white cotton blouse wrinkle-free and snowy white. "Oh, Jennie, I'm glad you're back. We have a visitor, someone I think you know."

"I'm really not dressed for company," Jennie said, eyeing the staircase and wondering if it would be rude to race up to the bathroom and slam the door.

"Oh, nonsense. I'm sure he's used to dusty ranchers. After all, his family is in ranching."

Curious now, Jennie allowed Rachel to snag her elbow and tug her toward the living room. "You say I know him? Who is he?"

"He's one of the Morgans from next door."

Jennie dug the heels of her Dingo boots into the hardwood floor, her stomach filling with a swarm of butterflies. Morgans? The only Morgan who'd ever been willing to step foot on the Flying W was—

A man stepped into view. His tall frame completely blocked the light from the picture windows behind him, throwing his face into shadow.

Jennie squinted, trying to make out his features.

"Hi, Jennie." The voice confirmed his identity in the first syllable.

Her mind scrambled to put words in her mouth while her stomach flip-flopped around the butterflies, as if trying to decide whether to leap for joy or upend from nausea. "Cameron."

Of all the people who might have come to visit, she never expected to see him. They hadn't spoken more than two words since their breakup, and so much had happened in between. With the Morgans and Wards feeling the way they did, she wouldn't think even the black sheep of the Morgan family would venture onto Ward property without a bulletproof vest.

Jennie moved around him, feeling dwarfed by his six-foot-three-inch frame. Her shoulder brushed against his arm, the scent of aftershave and leather assailing her nostrils, sending memories flittering through her jumbled thoughts. Why now? Why come back to the ranch now? Not that she couldn't handle it. She was a grown woman with a decade of experience behind her. Then why did she feel like the awkward teen she'd been when she'd fallen in love with Cameron Morgan?

Since then, she recognized it for what it had been— a teenage fantasy. She didn't love him anymore. There was nothing between them. He'd gone on to enter the army and she'd married Vance Franklin. Their lives had gone entirely different directions.

Once in the middle of the living room, she turned to see his face in the light.

Ten years.

Jennie was amazed at how much had changed in his face and how much was still the same Cameron. A few lines had appeared around his emerald-green eyes and his coal-black hair was shorter than when she'd dated him, probably a reflection of his time spent in the military. Such a shame, too. She used to love to run her fingers through his thick waves, making it stand on end. He'd tug her long, blond braid until her head tilted back and he could claim her lips in a scorching kiss. Jennie's heart hammered against her rib cage and she stammered, "You haven't changed a bit."

"Neither have you."

Jennie snorted. "You have that right. I'm still dusty and smell like a horse."

The lines around his eyes softened. "Better than the most expensive perfumes."

Jennie smiled, while fighting to resist falling into his deep green gaze. "You always were a charmer." He'd charmed her into loving him, and then he'd asked her to leave the only home she'd ever known and a father who needed her.

"And you were always so serious."

Ms. Blainey cleared her throat reminding Jennie she was still in the room. "I'll just go get a pitcher of lemonade while you two catch up."

A flare of panic ripped through Jennie. "Why don't you stay here and talk to Mr. Morgan while I get it?"

"I wouldn't hear of it. You've been out working all day. You're bound to be tired. You and Cameron go sit out on the porch." Ms. Blainey had a way of giving orders that didn't sound like orders, yet they were nonetheless effective.

Too tired to argue, Jennie led the way.

With Cameron following close on her heels, she felt a familiar tingle of awareness feathering across the base of her neck. So much had changed since he'd been gone, yet many things were still the same. Sure she'd been married and widowed, but the two families still hated each other and Cameron still wanted his life outside the ranch.

Since her mother had died, Jennie had promised to help her father with the ranch. As his only child, it was up to her to take care of her father, too. He needed someone to love him and see to his health. If she ever left, what would become of him?

In the meantime, what had become of her? A lonely widow who'd spent all her life working a ranch, for what?

She eased into a wooden rocker, stretching her booted feet out in front of her, hoping she appeared relaxed when every muscle in her body tensed to run. "So, Cameron, what brings you to the Flying W?" Deep down a part of her wanted his reason to be her. Her practical side knew better. If he'd wanted her, he'd have come home and fought for her ten years ago. Better still, he wouldn't have left.

For a long moment, he stared down at his hat and then he looked out across the foothills of the Rockies. "I think you and your father are in danger."

Chapter Two

Until he'd seen her, he had no idea how hard his mission would be. Covered in dust, her chambray shirt marred with stains from working out on the ranch, she couldn't have been more beautiful. So earthy, familiar and Jennie. The years had honed her body to tight athletic lines, her jeans rode loose on slim hips and her breasts were a bit fuller, fitting tightly against the worn cotton of her shirt. Her body had matured, but it was her eyes that had changed the most.

Instead of the open and happy harvest-gold they'd been in her youth, there were shadows beneath them and her expression was guarded. As it should be. After ten long years, having Cameron Morgan to show up her doorstep had to be a shock—probably not a pleasant one at that. The last time they'd been together, he'd given her a hard choice and she'd done what she always did, made the right decision.

Cameron shifted and straightened. All that was in the past. "You and your father are in danger," he repeated, his gaze scanning her face, searching for a hint of alarm, something to indicate her understanding of the gravity of his announcement.

She smiled, the curve of her lips easing the tension from her face. "Could you give me a few more details?" The teasing tone of her voice was the Jennie he remembered—the one he'd fallen in love with in his misspent youth.

"I work for Prescott Personal Securities out of Denver. We found evidence of a possible conspiracy to buy out landowners in this area."

"Buy out the Flying W?"

"Yes, and or the Bar M."

"Why?"

"We're not sure, but we think it's because of a recent discovery of oil reserves found in the area."

"So how does that put us in danger?" Jennie crossed her arms over her chest. "The Flying W isn't for sale."

"There is a possibility they'll play rough to get the land. Maybe even kill."

Jennie's eyes widened. "What proof do you have?"

"Two men who, because of their debts, were forced to sell their land and businesses for cash and a share in a blind trust. After they sold their property, both were murdered. Then we discovered a disk with coordinates of the dead men's property on it. We found the co-ordinates pointing to the border between the Flying W and the Bar M ranches right below the other two. We think it's the next target for acquisition. We have reason to believe whoever murdered the two men, might come after the Wards and the Morgans in order to acquire the land."

"What did your family say to this news?"

He shifted his hat in his hands. Why hadn't he stopped there first? "I haven't been there yet."

Her frown deepened. "Why?"

"Since there are five Morgans and only two Wards, I thought…" He stopped short of telling her why he'd dropped everything in Denver, shifting his current bodyguard gig to another agent just to race out to the Flying W.

"You thought we would be the easier target, didn't you?" Jennie's lips tightened into a thin line. She walked across the wooden decking, leaned a hip against the rail and stared out at the pine, fir and aspens sprinkled across the hillside.

In profile, her face appeared more drawn and worried than when he'd first seen her. The sudden urge to take that worry away from her pushed him forward and he took her hands. "Jennie, I work as a bodyguard. Let me protect you and your father."

She stared down at his hands and gently pulled hers free. "Dad will never go for it. He wouldn't tolerate a Morgan on Ward land for the amount of time it takes for him to say 'get the hell off.' You remember how it was. Nothing's changed."

Oh, he remembered all right. The nights he'd driven his truck up to the gate with the lights off and hiked up to the house just to see her. The stolen kisses behind the barn and the walks in the moonlight through the woods. He remembered all too well, as a familiar surge of longing threatened to muddy his thoughts. "I know, but we're both older and smarter than we were ten years ago. Surely he still isn't carrying a grudge against the Morgans."

Jennie's eyebrows rose. "Please. You're talking about Hank Ward, a man with the memory of an elephant. Whatever got them started on their silly feud is as fresh as the day it began. And you know as well as I, he's as stubborn as that old mule out in the pasture. No way he'll let you or anyone else protect him."

"You don't understand. These guys are playing for keeps. This is life or death."

"And every day on the ranch isn't life or death?"

When Cameron would have argued more, the sound of horses' hooves pounding toward them caught his attention. A sorrel horse with an empty saddle raced toward the house, ears pinned back and eyes wild. At the last moment, it veered toward the barn.

Jennie pushed away from the rail. "That's Red, Dad's horse." She was off the porch and running toward the barn, following the direction of the horse.

Cameron took off after her, his heart pounding against his ribs. Was he too late? Had whoever was responsible for all the killing already got to Hank Ward?

Before he cleared the side of the house, he heard the sound of a motorcycle engine revving.

Astride a four-wheeler, Jennie gunned the handle and spun around in the gravel headed straight for him.

"Wait!"

She dodged him and took off across the lawn and through the open gate leading out of the barnyard.

Cameron hopped on the back of another four-wheeler, kick-started the engine and spewed gravel in a tight turn.

Jennie was already halfway up the hillside before he passed through the gate. With a wide-open throttle, he sped after her, hoping his four-wheeling skills hadn't gotten too rusty to keep up.

"Slow down!" Cameron called out when he pulled up beside her. "You won't do him any good if you kill us both in the process."

"No way. He could be hurt." She twisted the

handle sending more gas to the engine and the vehicle leaped forward.

After several minutes of hard riding they topped the rise and descended into a mountain meadow filled with blue columbines and wild irises. The leaves on the aspens were a fresh spring green. If they weren't in such a hurry, Cameron would stop and soak up the beauty of being home in the mountains. He'd forgotten how much he missed the ranch.

But his focus remained on keeping Jennie in his sights. If he lost her, he might not find her in the vast-ness of the Flying W Ranch.

She topped another rise ahead of him, her vehicle slowing to a stop. Standing tall on her footrests, her head turned side to side.

Cameron pulled up beside her, set his cycle in neutral and rested his foot on the brake. Below them was an-other high mountain meadow. Cattle grazed, small brown specks amidst the lush green grasses.

"We moved these cattle up here yesterday. He and Rudy, our ranch hand, came up to check on them today and fix the fence in the far west corner of this meadow, past that line of trees."

From his perch atop the ridge, Cameron scanned the meadow. Not a human could be seen, only cows. "Come on." He shifted into gear and plunged down the side of the steep slope, dodging between the young junipers and firs dotting the east-facing slope.

Jennie followed and soon surged ahead. Skirting the herd, she led him toward a stand of old ponderosa pine. As she neared the far edge of the meadow, she slowed, allowing Cameron to close the distance and pull alongside.

As they entered the shadowy canopy of native forest, Cameron moved into the lead. Careful to dodge massive tree trunks, fallen brush and protruding roots, he hurried through the clump of trees to the other side. He could see sunlight ahead, and was that movement?

"Hey!" A voice carried to him above the roar of the motorcycle engine. At the edge of the clearing stood a young man Cameron didn't recognize. Leaning against him with his arm draped over the young man was Hank Ward, an angry scowl marring his face.

Jennie skidded to a stop ten feet from her father. She killed the engine, leaped off the seat and raced to his side. "Dad, what happened?"

"Fell off my horse," he grumbled.

The young man frowned. "He didn't just fall off his horse."

Hank glared at him, his expression fierce. "Hold your tongue, boy."

"What happened, Rudy?" Jennie asked.

Rudy glanced at Jennie, a worried frown on his young forehead. "Someone fired a shot at him. It hit the ground in front of Red's hooves. Spooked him so bad, he dumped Hank on the ground and lit out like his tail was on fire."

"Damned horse reared so fast…" Hank shook his head. "I haven't fallen off my horse since I don't re-member when."

"Where are you hurt?" Jennie scanned her father from head to toe.

"Only my tailbone, my ankle and my pride."

"It's his left ankle. He couldn't get it into the stirrup to mount and he couldn't balance on his sore ankle long enough to get on my horse from the other side."

"I can walk just fine," Hank groused.

"Yeah? How about you prove it?" Rudy lifted Hank's arm from around his neck, but Hank stopped him.

"Okay, okay. So my ankle's botherin' me. I'd have been all right if my danged horse hadn't lit out of here."

Cameron finally stepped forward. "Any idea which direction the bullet came from, Mr. Ward?"

Hank focused on Cameron as if it was the first time he'd noticed him. "Who are you?"

After ten years away from the ranch, six of which had been spent in the Army Rangers, Cameron had matured and changed.

Hank hadn't recognized him, yet.

With a deep breath he stepped closer, ready for the worst. "Cameron Morgan, sir."

Dead silence ensued. Even the birds stopped chirping for the five long seconds it took for Hank's face to flush an angry red. "What the hell are you doing on my property?"

As ANGER FIRED through her blood, Jennie stepped between them. Nothing ever changed. Why did her father have to be so pigheaded? "Dad, you're hurt. Let's get you back to the house. We can discuss everything there."

"I'm not goin' anywhere with a Morgan."

"The hell you're not." Jennie's lips tightened. She might have acquiesced when she was eighteen, but at twenty-eight she'd lived a tough life on the ranch. She'd learned a lot about managing men by riding side by side with the ranch hands. Her father was a man, and a very ornery one at that. She wasn't taking any of his bull this time. "You might be my father, but I'm not putting up with stubborn stupidity. Rudy, get him to the back of my four-wheeler. I'll take him to the house."

"Here, let me help." Cameron moved to one side of Hank.

The older man glared at him. "I don't need the help of a Morgan. They've caused me nothin' but trouble. And you should know that best." He shot a hard stare at Jennie.

Jennie hid a smile when Cameron ignored him and took his elbow, helping him to the vehicle.

Hank winced as he straddled the seat and eased down. "Danged tailbone hurts like hell. You drive slow, Jen."

"I will, Dad." Jennie slid onto the seat in front of her father.

"Like to know who shot at me."

A cold, hard lump settled in Jennie's stomach, and she glanced at Cameron. "So would we."

Chapter Three

"What do you mean someone might be trying to kill me?" Hank sat bolt upright in his recliner, his face creasing in pain. He immediately eased back, relieving the pressure on his tailbone. "Shoot fire, someone almost did today. But that doesn't mean I gotta run scared. A Ward doesn't run." He aimed a narrow look at Cameron as if to say some Morgans ran.

Jennie had called a meeting of the entire crew in the living room of the ranch house, against her father's wishes.

Stan stood beside her father, Rudy sat on a hard-backed wooden chair and Doug stood near the door, looking as if being inside the living room of the house was as foreign as stepping into a queen's palace.

"If what Cameron is telling us is true," Jennie argued, "we could all be in danger. It's only fair to inform everyone of what might happen."

"I say it's all a bunch of scare tactics by your body-guard agency to get folks out here to hire you on." Hank lifted up to adjust the pillow beneath his bottom. "Damn tailbone. I should be out chasing after the son-of-a—"

"Hank Ward, watch your mouth." Ms. Blainey swept through the room carrying a tray with drinks.

"Sir, I'll be working on my own time for this case," Cameron stated. "You won't be required to pay anything. Prescott Personal Securities is in this no matter whether they get paid or not. Two of our agents have already been involved and almost killed trying to figure out what's going on and who killed the CEOs."

When the older woman fussed over the pillows behind Hank's head, he waved her away. "Leave it, woman. I can do for myself."

"I can see that," Ms. Blainey said, a smile twitching at the corners of her mouth, undeterred by Hank's surly disposition.

The owner of the Flying W focused his attention on Cameron. "Why don't you go put a tail on the Russian mob, or figure out who owns that blind trust and leave us alone?"

"I understand your frustration, sir," Cameron stated. "But this could be a very dangerous situation for you and Jennie."

Jennie watched the two men posturing in the living room. If Cameron hoped to win her father over, he had to be the sound and rational one. Hank could get downright blustery and mean. As the younger man, and a Morgan, he had to prove to the old coot he could keep his cool, no matter what was thrown at him.

"We don't have any evidence other than a land coordinate found on a disk full of other land coordinates, two of which match the land formerly owned by dead men," Cameron explained again. "There are not enough hard facts to get the police interested. We're not sure of the motive for the killings, but we think you might be in danger."

"Sounds like you don't know much." Hank's

words were spoken with harsh undertones, clearly meant as an insult.

Cameron nodded, a serious frown bringing his eyebrows together. "That's right, sir. We don't know enough. But we're fairly certain that whatever happens next will happen to either the Wards or the Morgans."

Hank slapped the arm of his chair. "Then go warn your family. We'll take care of our own."

"I will, sir." Cameron stepped forward, his jaw hardening. "When I'm done here."

The older man glared at Cameron. "You're done as far as I'm concerned."

Jennie could have kicked her father. "If you'd stop being such a horse's behind, you might listen to the rest. Cameron's offered to stay on and be our bodyguard until this thing blows over."

Hank barked out a cross between a snort and laughter. The movement jostled his body and a moan escaped his lips. He winced and shifted on the pillow. "A Morgan playing bodyguard to a Ward? No way. Especially not to my Jennie. That's kinda like the fox guarding the henhouse, if you ask me. I won't have you breakin' her heart all over again."

Heat burned a path up Jennie's neck to fill her cheeks. "Dad, that was a long time ago. It's not as if he'll break anybody's heart. There's nothing between the two of us anymore." She could feel the warmth of Cameron's gaze on her, but she hesitated to face him.

After a deep breath, she turned toward the first man she'd ever loved and leveled a stare at him, telling herself she believed what she'd said—there was nothing left between them. He'd left ten years ago. She'd married after he left and the rest was history.

Relationships hurt, sometimes physically, and she wanted no part of that. She wasn't interested in starting something with Cameron Morgan at all. Not one bit. A little voice in the back of her consciousness whispered, "Liar." Squelching that voice, she said, "There's nothing between us, isn't that right?"

Cameron caught her gaze and held it for a long moment before he answered. "That's right."

Despite her conviction, the ache in her belly left her empty. She knew better than anyone relationships didn't always work out. She and Cameron never really had a chance, not with the way their families felt about each other and the way Cameron felt about staying on the ranch. The circumstances hadn't changed. The Morgans still hated the Wards and the feeling was mutual on her father's part.

"I don't care whether or not there's anything goin' on between you two," Hank said. "Strike that. Yes I do care, but that's beside the point. We can take care of our own."

"Bull." Jennie propped her hands on her hips. "You won't be getting around for at least two weeks on that ankle. We only have three men to work the ranch. If we pull them to baby-sit you and me, who will take care of the livestock?"

Her father opened his mouth, closed it, opened it again and then crossed his arms over his chest. "I don't want a Morgan on my property."

Jennie crossed her own arms over her chest like her father and leveled a fierce look at him. "Tough. How do you explain that snake in the feed bin last week?"

"Hungry snake?" Hank countered.

Jennie rolled her eyes. "You know as well as everyone else, those lids are always on tight to keep the mice out."

"Someone probably forgot to put it back." Hank's voice was more belligerent than convincing.

"Do you ever leave the lid off the feed bins Stan, Rudy, Doug?" She glanced at each man one at a time. Each shook his head and mumbled, "No, ma'am." Doug fidgeted with the straw cowboy hat he held between his large calloused hands, his gaze darting toward the door every few minutes.

Perhaps having the hands in on the discussion wasn't the right way to handle the problem. They liked their solitude, especially Doug, the loner.

"You should have seen Miss Jennie when she saw that snake." Rudy grinned at Cameron. "Hit it with her first shot—using a pistol, no less."

Refusing to be sidetracked, Jennie brought up the issue she'd discovered that morning. "What about the razor blade in my saddle?"

Cameron's eyes widened. "Razor blade?"

Jennie nodded.

Her father didn't have an answer for that one. His face set in a stubborn scowl. "I won't have a Morgan on my property."

"Seems like you're in no condition to disagree." Jennie leaned close to her father, her face in an equally stubborn scowl. "If I say he stays, he stays."

Hank's cheeks burned red beneath the tanned, leatherlike skin. "This is my ranch, girl. I make the decisions."

"Oh quit your bellyaching, Hank, and take these painkillers." Rachel Blainey was back in the room, handing Hank two tablets and a tall glass of lemonade. "Jennie's right. You need help, whether you like it or not. Cameron's offering at no cost. You'd be a fool to refuse."

"What's with the women in this house? Isn't a man's home supposed to be his castle?" Hank tossed the pills to the back of his throat and swallowed a gulp of lemonade. "I will not be overruled by a couple of women. I'm the boss and I can fire you if I want." His bluster faded a bit when Rachel winced.

The older woman stood firm. "You have that right, but you'd be an even bigger fool to do it. Who would cook the meals?"

He nodded toward Jennie.

She shook her head and smiled. "You want to live to be eighty, don't you?"

"Then Rudy can learn to cook."

Rudy backed away, his hands held up. "Oh no, not me. I wouldn't know a pan from a skillet. Besides, who would take care of the animals?"

Hank turned a hopeful look on Stan Keller, his foreman and longtime friend.

Stan shook his head. "All I can cook is canned beans and weenies. Care to eat that three times a day, seven days a week? I like Ms. Rachel's cookin'. I like it enough I'd consider quittin' if she was to up and leave."

Hank's brows rose high on his forehead. "You won't leave me. You're practically family."

"So's Ms. Rachel," Stan replied.

Hank snorted and stared around at the set faces. "Overruled on my on property. I don't like it." He pounded the arm of the recliner with his palm. "Morgans don't belong on the Flying W."

"Says who?" Jennie asked. "Whatever's stuck in your craw better just get unstuck. He's staying."

WITH ONE HURDLE CROSSED, Cameron headed to the small town of Dry Wash to inform the sheriff of the attempts on the Wards' lives. After the sheriff promised to make a trek out to the Flying W for further information, Cameron left for the Bar M Ranch to warn his family of the trouble headed their way. Frankly, he didn't expect any warmer welcome from some of his relatives than he'd got from Hank Ward.

When he pulled into the yard and parked, a young woman with auburn hair and bright green eyes flew off the porch and attacked him before he could shut his truck door. "Whoa, wait a minute there, Molly."

"Cameron!" She hugged him around the middle so hard he could barely breathe. "I can't believe it's you. Let me look at you." She leaned back, her arms still around his waist, tears shimmering in her eyes. "You're back and you look great."

"Hey, carrot." He ruffled his sister's hair and set her away. "Let me get a look at you. What's it been— two years?"

"Make that three." Molly tossed her bright auburn hair, her green eyes flashing.

Cameron marveled at how much she looked like their mother. Happy and sweet—the spitting image of Emma Morgan.

"Last time I saw you was at my high school graduation." Her gaze was accusing, tempered by her ready smile.

"Aren't you supposed to be at college?"

"I finished my last exam two days ago. I couldn't wait to come home, I've been so homesick."

Cameron knew that feeling. "Denver's not that far, knucklehead." He rubbed the top of her head as he'd done when she was no taller then his belt buckle. Now, she stood up to his chin at five feet ten. No longer a gangly teen, she'd filled out in all the right places. "Hey, when did you grow up?"

She punched him in the belly and then raised the same hand to straighten her hair. "A long time ago, doofus. Come on, I know Mom will be over the moon to see you." She hooked her arm around his waist and led him up the steps and through the front door of the two-story stone-and-cedar ranch house.

How many times had he hopped up those same steps two at a time growing up on the Bar M Ranch? Back then, he didn't have a care in the world, never thinking past dinner or riding his favorite horse the next day. His chest tightened. He'd missed home.

Then why the heck had he stayed away so long?

"Hey, brother." The sound of his older brother's voice reminded him of the reason why. Logan Morgan stepped through the door leading to the kitchen. Instead of the hug Molly had given him, Logan held out his hand. "Been a while."

Cameron grasped his brother's hand and shook, his grip strong. *A measure of a man's worth,* his father would say. "Molly was just reminding me how long." Where had the easy camaraderie they'd shared in their youth gone? For over a decade, Logan had been cold and distant to him. Ever since he'd started seeing Jennie Ward. He might as well have committed treason or murder by the way Logan and his father treated him.

If not for his mother and Molly, Cameron wouldn't have returned to the Bar M. Though he loved the land and enjoyed working with his hands, he'd been a stranger in his own home, ostracized for his association with the Ward girl, as they loved to call her. Even after he'd left to join the army and Jennie had refused to leave with him, his father and brother hadn't forgiven him or welcomed him back into the fold. Old wounds only seemed to fester and grow deeper.

"What brings you home?" Logan dropped his hand and hooked a thumb in his belt loop.

"Do I have to have a reason other than to see my family?" Cameron asked.

"Usually. Molly's graduation and Mom's surgery were the only times you've been home over the past five years. We're all healthy here and Molly doesn't graduate college for another year or more." Logan's brows rose over deep brown eyes. Where Molly favored their mother, Logan was a mirror image of their father in looks and attitude.

Cameron fell in the middle. Black hair like his father, green eyes like his mother and somewhere in the center between the rigid views of Tom Morgan and the full-time mediator who was Emma Morgan. He was saved from an answer by a whirlwind of denim and chambray.

"Cam, honey! I can't believe it's you." Emma Morgan strode into the room, her Dingo-booted feet tapping against the hardwood floors. The dust in her hair made it hard to determine how much was dust and how much of her auburn curls had turned gray. Without hesitation, she pulled him into her arms and hugged him close. "God, I missed you." She held on for longer than usual until Logan cleared his throat, ending the touching reunion.

Cameron could have gone on a lot longer hugging his mother. Until she'd come through the door, he hadn't realized how much he'd missed her smile and her down-

to-earth ways. What you saw was what you got with
Emma Morgan. She didn't have a secretive, mean or tricky
bone in her body. Molly was just like her and he loved
them both all the more. "Hi, Mom. I missed you, too."

When she pulled away, a tear made a trail down the
dust on her cheeks. Reaching up she brushed it away.
"Now see there, you'll have me bawling like a newborn
calf if you don't watch out."

Fighting the lump lodged in his throat, Cameron
smiled. "Maybe I'll join you."

"While you two are crying, I have horses to tend."
Logan left without looking back.

Emma's gaze followed him. "I don't understand that
boy."

Her "boy" was all of thirty and then some.

"He needs to fall in love or something to take the
edge off," Molly said.

"Wish he would. Might bring him down a peg or two
to meet his match in a female." Emma's attention
returned to Cameron, her smile returning with it. "It's
good to have you home, son."

"It's good to be back." Despite the bad feelings between him and the male members of his family,
Cameron really was glad to be back in the mountains.
"What have you been up to?" He stood back and stared
down at her dusty jeans.

His mother laughed. "I was lunging a new filly I
think will make a good mount for Molly. Logan's set
to break her next week." Emma Morgan didn't apolo-
gize for her appearance and Cameron didn't expect her
to. From the time she could walk she'd been riding
horses. Having children or a husband didn't slow her
down for a minute. In this respect, Molly was slightly

different. Although an accomplished barrel racer, Molly wasn't as passionate about riding horses as her mother, preferring to go to college and learn more about what goes into making a good healthy horse.

"Did Molly tell you she made Dean's List again?" his mother asked.

Cameron clapped a hand to his sister's back. "So, does that make every semester so far?"

Molly shrugged, but a grin lit her freckled face. "Yeah. Gotta have top grades to get into Colorado State's Veterinary School."

"You'll make it at that rate." His sister was smart and determined to succeed, like every other Morgan on the ranch. They'd been raised to win. He wondered where he'd have been if he'd taken the football scholarship to University of Colorado, instead of tossing it all and joining the army. Not that he regretted joining the army. He'd learned more in his six years as a Ranger than if he'd spent the same six in college.

"Molly, why don't you get your brother something to drink?"

"What'll you have? Coffee, soda or beer? I'm legal now, you know." Already on her way to the kitchen, Molly smiled over her shoulder. "What'll it be?"

"Water would be great."

As soon as Molly left the living room, Emma Morgan's smile turned downward. "What's wrong?"

His mother could always see through him and he wasn't going to stall her as he had Logan. His mother would listen and if he hoped to get his father to hear and understand, he had to convince her of the danger and the need to be careful. "Prescott Personal Securities has come across some kind of conspiracy and we think it's headed toward the border of the Bar M and the Flying W."

The light died in her eyes and her lips thinned into a straight line. "Tell me about it."

Molly returned with a glass of water and they sat on the brown leather chairs around the stone fireplace. For the next twenty minutes Cameron told them what he'd told the Wards.

"Wow. It's all kinda scary. Do you really think we're in danger?" Molly asked, a frown mixing the freckles on her brow.

Cameron nodded, his gaze focused on his mother's worried, dust-streaked face. "Yes, ma'am."

"I know you wouldn't have come out to tell us if you didn't mean it." His mother patted his hand. "I'm just sorry it has to be bad news that brings you out." She sighed. "Now, all we have to do is convince the men. I'm going to clean up for dinner. Your father will be in at any moment. Logan's probably clued him in that you're here."

As soon as his mother left the room, Molly pounced on him with questions of her own. "How was Jennie? I haven't seen her in so long. Are you two going to start seeing each other again? I think this whole feud mess is just stupid and we should tell Dad to just get over it."

"Tell Dad to get over what?" The deep, rich timbre of Tom Morgan's voice filled the room all the way to the exposed rough-hewn timbers in the cathedral ceiling.

Cameron rose from the chair and almost laughed out loud at his sister.

Molly's eyes widened and she gulped. She stood and hooked Cameron's arm, turning him to face his father. "Dad, look who's here."

His father dipped his head. "Son." No hug, no smile. Just one word and it was as cold as a blue norther screaming down off the slopes. What did it take to melt the mountain of ice around his father's heart? Would he ever forgive him for making his own choices and meet him halfway?

"Hi, Dad." Not for the first time, Cameron regretted the loss of the closeness they'd shared in his teens. Cameron had never understood the rift between Tom Morgan and Hank Ward, and his father hadn't bothered to enlighten him. The feud resulting from the rift had been the major reason he'd left everything he loved behind—the Bar M Ranch, his family and Jennie.

Logan entered behind his father and stood beside him.

"What brings you out of the big city?" His father slapped his hat against his thigh, a thin cloud of dust rising from the denim.

Cameron knew better than to sugarcoat anything for his father. "Trouble."

Logan snorted. "Figures."

"What kind of trouble?" his father asked.

"I think someone might be out to hurt either the Morgans or the Wards. Maybe both. I just came over from the Flying W. Someone took a shot at Hank Ward."

"Good, the old man probably deserves it," Logan said.

But his father didn't respond immediately. His jaw tightened and his brown eyes burned. "You went to the Flying W instead of telling your own family first?"

He should have expected his father to react that way. Nevertheless the older man's words rubbed Cameron wrong. Jennie had been his sweetheart, his first love.

Tom Morgan had never reconciled himself to Cameron seeing Jennie and viewed his association as defection to the other side.

Cameron opened his mouth to explain his reasoning and thought better of it. "Yes. I stopped at the Flying W."

"You always were the black sheep. I never could get it through your head that Morgans and Wards don't mix."

Molly blew out a loud sigh and let go of Cameron's arm. "While you men are conducting your pissing contest, I'll put fresh sheets on the bed in your old room."

"Don't bother, Molly." Cameron's gaze met his father's. "I'll be staying at the Flying W."

Chapter Four

Cameron held his breath, maintaining a poker face as his father's chest filled like an overextended balloon. Instead of the explosive tirade Cameron fully expected, Tom Morgan spun on his booted heel and left the house, the door slamming behind him.

Logan shot an intense glare at Cameron and followed his father out the door, leaving Cameron and the women standing in their wake.

Cameron's mother expelled a long breath and forced a smile. "Well, that went over well, now didn't it?" She clapped her hands together. "What can I get you? Do you want to take your saddle? You might need it over there."

"If you still have it, that would be great." Cameron crossed the room and stood in front of his mother. "I'm sorry if I've made things uncomfortable for you and Molly."

"And I'm sorry your father is so bullheaded." She smiled up at him and touched a hand to his cheek. "I'm glad to see you, son. Don't let your father's attitude make you think any differently."

He touched a hand to hers, pressing her cool, dry

fingers to his heated skin. "You understand why I have to go to the Flying W, don't you?"

"Yes."

Molly stepped up beside him. "Me, too."

"There's another man from the agency, Jack Sanders, who is due to come out to stay with you and provide you with protection. I told him to give it a day before he came." He sighed. "See what you can do to convince him." Cameron jerked his head in the direction his father had gone.

"I will. If nothing else, we'll keep Jack around the house for Molly and me."

"Not that you can't handle a gun or horse better than any man in the county. Of that I have no doubt. But it helps to have another pair of eyes looking out for you, especially while you're working."

"Thanks, Cam." His mother pushed her hair back off her dirty face and smiled. "You better get that saddle and hightail it back to the Ward's place. Hate to think of Hank being laid up and Jennie fending for herself."

Cameron turned to go and thought again. "Mom, what happened to make Dad hate Hank Ward so much? No one's ever bothered to tell us."

His mother drew in a deep breath and let it out slowly. "It's a touchy subject."

"Considering what's going on, now might be the time to tell me about it."

She glanced toward the windows, her face drawn and looking far older than a moment earlier. "I'm not sure I want to dredge up the past. Some things are best left alone. But, let me think about it." Then she gave him a weak smile.

"Fair enough." Disappointed, Cameron knew he

couldn't push for the information. He'd planted the seed, now he'd stand back and wait to see if it grew into enough trust that his mother would tell him what he'd always wanted to know.

Molly grabbed his arm and dragged him toward the door. "I'll help you find the saddle. I've reorganized the tack room in the barn. Come on."

"See you soon?" Cameron waved a hand toward his mother.

She nodded. "Count on it."

When Molly had him outside, she dropped his arm. "I thought I'd never get you out of the house. Mom doesn't like to talk about the feud and the Wards. There's a lot of bad water under that bridge."

"Why? Do you know anything about it?"

"All I know is that I heard Mom and Dad arguing one night when I was little. I remember hearing Dad shouting something about Hank and Louise and him being wrong about something."

Cameron planted his heels in the dirt and turned to Molly. "Wrong about what?"

His sister shrugged. "I don't know. I was too little to understand, I just remembered the names."

"It would help to know what's gone on between them to create such a rift they haven't talked in over thirty years."

"I'll dig around and see what I can find out."

With a crooked finger, Cameron chucked his sister beneath her chin. "In the meantime, watch out for yourself. Never go out alone."

Her lips twisted. "Give me a break. I can take care of myself."

He grabbed her shoulders and forced her to look

him in the eye. "Promise me." His words weren't a request.

For a moment, she hesitated, a stubborn frown marring her freckled forehead. Her face softened and she nodded. "Okay, I'll be careful and never go out on my own. There, does that make you feel better?"

He loosened his grip and let her go. "Yes."

A blond-haired cowboy Cameron didn't recognize led a bay gelding out of the barn and stopped to adjust the cinch strap. When he looked up, he swept the straw cowboy hat from his head and smiled. "Hi, Miss Molly."

Molly's face transformed from serious to all smiles. "Hi, Brad." Her cheeks turned an attractive shade of pink and she clutched at Cameron's arm, dragging him forward. "Cameron, meet Brad Carter. He's one of the new hands Dad hired a couple weeks ago to help out while Ty's out of commission. Brad, this is my brother, Cameron."

Brad held out a hand and shook Cameron's. "Molly's told me all about you. Said you were in the army."

"That's right." Cameron's gaze raked over the man from his crisp blue chambray shirt down to his ostrich skin boots. "You been a ranch hand before?"

Brad laughed. "I did some ranching out in Montana, then tried my hand in Denver real estate. Found out I liked working with animals better than people. It had been a while since I'd been on a horse, but your father gave me the benefit of the doubt. I've been here ever since."

"Don't let him fool you. He's great on a horse and good with cattle."

"You staying in Ty's quarters?" Cameron asked.

"No, I have a room over Mrs. Green's garage in Dry Wash."

Cameron nodded, suspicious of any stranger, but not yet alarmed. "Nice to meet you."

"If you'll pardon me. I have a fence to mend out on the south border." He glanced at the sun angling toward the horizon. "I'd better get going if I want to get back before dark." Brad swung up into the saddle, tipped his cowboy hat at Molly and touched his heels to the horse's flanks.

"What happened to Ty?" Cameron and Ty Masters had played football at the same high school and dated some of the same girls. When Cameron left to join the army, his father had hired Ty to shoulder the workload Cameron's departure left.

"He was thrown by his horse and broke his leg pretty bad. Pretty freak accident. Said his horse stumbled coming down a hill he'd ridden more times that he can remember and never had a problem with before. If Mom hadn't been out riding, he'd have been there awhile. He's been laid up for three weeks and has another three to go before he gets out of the cast. Dad thinks it'll take him another month or so before he's up to riding. Maybe longer. That's why he hired Brad."

Cameron's brows dipped. "How come I haven't heard about Ty?"

"Must have slipped my mind during all my finals at school." She swatted at his arm. "If you'd wanted to know, you could have called Mom for your personal news service. I'm only here on vacation now."

"I keep forgetting you're a college student. I still think of you as that gawky girl with the ponytail always following me around."

"I haven't been that for a while now."

"I noticed." Cameron stared out at the pastures and surrounding hills, speckled with evergreens and aspens.

The clean, fresh air lightly scented with the distinctive aroma of spruce filled his lungs. Topped with sparkling blue skies, the scenery tugged at his heart. He'd always loved the ranch, loved working with the animals and probably would have stayed on the way his brother Logan did, had he not fallen in love with the neighbor girl and stirred up a hornets' nest of hatred.

"So, how's Jennie?" Molly might as well have been reading his mind.

Her question jolted him back to the present and his purpose for being there. "She's good." Beautiful as ever and just as stubborn as he remembered. If not for the dark smudges beneath her eyes, he'd say she hadn't changed a bit.

Molly hooked her thumbs in her belt loops as she walked. "She's had a tough time of it."

"How so?"

"Stuck out on that ranch, not dating. I hope she wises up and gets a life before she's too old to enjoy it."

"It's her choice."

"Maybe so." Molly ambled toward the barn, kicking at the gravel with her dingo boots. "From what I understand, she's pretty bitter about marriage and men in general."

Despite his resolve to stay out of Jennie's business, he couldn't help asking, "Why?"

Molly glanced up at him, her eyes wide. "You don't know?"

"Know what?"

"Gosh, that's such old news I thought for sure you'd have heard it long before I did. I was only eleven at the time."

Cameron stopped outside the barn door and grasped

Molly's arms, his patience for guessing at an end. "What are you talking about? Why is Jennie down on men and marriage?"

"Her ex-husband. I thought you knew."

Cameron knew Jennie had married shortly after he left. Hurt by how quickly she'd got over him, he'd cut ties and moved on with his life in the military.

Molly shook off her brother's hands. "He abused her. Slapped her around mentally and physically. That's why she filed for divorce." Molly's lips twisted. "The bastard really messed her up. He deserved to die."

"What do you mean?"

"Vance Franklin died in a car wreck after Jennie filed for divorce."

Cameron withheld comment, holding back the string of curses he wanted to let loose. How could any man be cruel enough to hit a woman? And to hit Jennie, that was unconscionable. If Vance were still alive, he'd take the man out. He agreed with his sister, the man deserved to die.

Had he only known Jennie was in trouble back then…

He knew she was in trouble now and he'd do everything in his power to keep her safe.

MEN DIDN'T MAKE good patients—especially hardworking ranch owners who didn't know the meaning of downtime. For most of the afternoon, Jennie helped Ms. Blainey fetch and carry for her cranky father. Unused to being trapped indoors, Hank groused and hollered over every little thing.

By dusk, Jennie was fit to be tied. If she didn't get

out of the house soon, she'd go nuts. The horses needed feed and Lady needed her dressing changed.

Cameron had told her to stay inside until he returned, but the sun tipped toward the horizon and he still wasn't back. Unwilling to stay indoors a moment longer, she took a deep breath, opened the door and stepped out onto the porch. A quick glance around had her laughing at herself. What did she expect? The bogeyman?

Shaking her shoulders loose of the tension building there all day, Jennie strode toward the barn, a trip she'd made a million times since the day she was born. Why should today be any different?

Because someone had taken a potshot at her father? Or because Cameron Morgan might show up at any time? What was she more frightened of? The unknown threat or the known?

Ten years had passed since she'd seen Cameron. The years had hardened him into a man, not the teenager she'd fallen in love with. Had she made a mistake taking him on as a bodyguard? Did she still harbor feelings toward this man?

Jennie jerked open the barn door and entered its dark interior. Stan, Doug and Rudy were out working the fences. They would be back at dark, hungry and tired—too tired to deal with the stabled horses. All the more reason for her to feed, water and apply first aid where needed. When Jennie flipped the light switch, nothing happened.

At first, Jennie thought nothing of it. The wiring was old and occasionally a breaker tripped. The near dark didn't bother her. She knew the barn like the back of her hand and her eyes were beginning to adjust to the dim interior.

Lady whinnied from her corner stall, the sound high-pitched and accompanied by a hoof slammed against the wooden sides of her stall.

"What's wrong, girl? Didn't I get out here soon enough for your liking?" As Jennie made her way through the shadowy barn, she talked to the horse in a soft, reassuring voice. When she reached out to open the large trash can housing the grain she fed the horses, she waited a moment before sticking her hand inside, remembering the surprise snake her father had found a few days prior. Just as she reached for the feed bucket, something moved at the corner of her peripheral vision, and it wasn't a horse.

Before she could shout or even turn, something hard hit the back of her head.

Pain knifed through her, she crumpled to her knees, and her world went fuzzy around the edges.

Jennie fell to the ground, her brain working, albeit not well. If the attacker thought she was unconscious, perhaps he'd leave her alone. She lay still, her head pounding, fighting back the inky blackness threatening to engulf her.

Footsteps sounded on the hard-packed earth, headed for the front entrance to the barn.

Crawling low behind the feed bin, Jennie pulled herself to her knees and waited for her attacker's return. She heard the sound of the large wooden door closing with a click. Had he gone? Was it safe to come out?

Then footsteps ran across the floor in front of the feed barrel. Jennie hunkered low, ready to jump out and face the menace. She strained to see in the near dark, only managing to catch a glimpse of the shadowy figure racing for the back door. Something flashed in the dark. A spark?

The scent of sulfur and smoke filled the air as if a whole book of matches had been lit.

Jennie jumped up and ran after the man, her head swimming, making her progress wobbly at best. She had to stop him from dropping the fire inside the barn. The place would burn so fast there wouldn't be time for the Dry Wash's Volunteer Fire Department to respond.

The burning bundle flew toward the corner where stacked hay bales sat. The man hustled through the door and out of the barn so fast Jennie didn't have a chance to catch up to him. As she reached for the back door, the sound of a horse's hooves pounding against the dirt let her know he'd gotten away, but maybe she could see who it was.

She tried the door. It didn't budge.

Flames rose behind her, dancing dangerously close to her back. Jennie leaped out of the way and grabbed for a horse blanket. Using the blanket, she beat at the flames, trying to put out the fire now firmly entrenched in the straw bales. As smoke filled the interior, Jennie realized she couldn't put the fire out on her own. She had to get Lady out and go for help.

As she ran for Lady's stall, dry, scorching heat flared behind her, smoke rose choking off her air.

Inside the horse's stall, Lady screamed and reared, slamming against the wooden walls.

Jennie slid open the gate and grabbed for the horse's halter. Smoke filled her lungs and she gave in to a bout of coughing. Then, pulling her shirt over her mouth, she ran for the front door, dragging the frantic horse behind her. She had to get her out, quickly, before the smoke overcame them both.

With her arm stretched out in front of her, she felt

her way through the smoke. Once she located the door, she pushed the latch and leaned her weight into the heavy wood. It still wouldn't budge. She pushed again, putting all her strength into the effort.

The front and back doors didn't move. It had been locked with her inside.

The stack of hay became a towering inferno shooting flames up the beams into the dry wooden flooring of the loft, also full of dry hay bales.

With heat scorching her skin and lungs, Jennie sank to her knees, trying to get as low as possible. She pulled hard on Lady's head to move the horse's nostrils closer to the ground and away from the rising smoke.

With the back entrance blocked by flame, all Jennie could do was beat against the door, screaming until her voice cracked and her lungs were raw and scratchy from smoke.

Chapter Five

Molly's revelation about Jennie's marriage roiled around in Cameron's thoughts as he traveled the road between the Morgan and the Ward ranches. How could Jennie put up with the abuse? She'd been a firebrand when he'd known her—full of confidence and a strong sense of family. How had he missed this piece of news? Molly had always kept him up to date on the goings-on in the small community of Dry Wash. Had she been too young to understand Jennie's plight at the time?

All Cameron had heard was that she'd married shortly after he'd left for the military.

Shadows thickened as he rounded the curve in the road leading to the Flying W ranch house. Nearing the ranch, he caught a glimpse of flames and black smoke billowing above the treetops.

What the hell? His foot slammed the accelerator to the floorboard and the truck leaped forward, eating up the remaining distance.

By the amount of smoke filling the sky, the fire must be big and it appeared to be coming from the back side of the house. Cameron's chest squeezed. Jennie was in the house with her father. Had the same person who'd taken a shot at Hank come back to finish the job?

Cameron slammed a palm to the steering wheel. Why had he thought it all right to leave the Wards without his protection? These criminals had already killed two people and probably others he didn't know about.

As he skidded around the side of the house, he noted that it wasn't the house on fire, but the barn. For a moment, Cameron breathed a sigh of relief. Jennie was given strict instructions to stay in the house with her father.

When Ms. Blainey burst out of the kitchen door and headed toward the burning barn, Cameron knew instinctively that Jennie hadn't followed instructions.

Gunning the accelerator, Cameron raced the truck toward the inferno, reaching the barn a couple yards ahead of Ms. Blainey. He dropped out of the driver's seat and ran for the barn door. "Anyone in there?" he called out to the woman behind him.

"Jennie!" Ms. Blainey kept running until she skidded to a halt in front of the barn door. "Jennie came outside a few minutes ago to take care of the horses. Oh God! She's in there!"

"Help!" A faint cry sounded through the thick wooden door, followed by a horse's panicked scream.

Cameron reached for the handle on the barn door and pulled. It didn't budge. Something was keeping the door from opening. Flames rose from the rooftop and timbers crashed downward. He didn't have time to waste. "Stand back from the door, Jennie."

A hacking cough preceded her answer. "Okay."

"What are you going to do? We can't leave her in there." Ms. Blainey reached for the door and jiggled the handle.

Cameron didn't take time to respond. He raced for his truck, swung up into the driver's seat and shoved the gear into drive. "Call 9-1-1!" he yelled through the open window.

Ms. Blainey's eyes widened and she ran for the house.

Sending a silent prayer heavenward that Jennie managed to get herself and the horse out of the way, Cameron goosed the engine. Then, jamming his foot to the accelerator, he sent the truck barreling forward, ramming through the heavy doors, creating a truck-sized hole through splintered wood.

As quickly as he burst into the barn, Cameron slammed the gears into reverse and pulled out to the screeching sound of wood on metal. Smoke billowed out of the new opening, the flames rising higher into the sky.

Before he could open his door, a horse leaped out of the raging inferno through the jagged gap in the barn door, narrowly missing the truck.

Cameron wrenched his door open and leaped to the ground running. Jennie was still in there. Pulling his shirt up over his mouth and nose, he ducked low and entered the burning shell. Heat seared his skin and the smoke stung his eyes to tears. He held his breath, reluctant to breathe in the dense smoke filling the structure. Dropping to a low crouch, he felt his way to the left of the barn door.

Behind the battered remains of the entrance, he found Jennie, slumped against the hard-packed dirt floor. When he tapped her shoulder, she didn't respond. Was he too late? Had she been claimed by smoke inhalation? Cameron didn't take the time to check. As heat and flame crept closer, he scooped her up in his arms and carried her out of the blaze. He ran until he was back at the house.

Once on the porch, he laid her down and crouched next to her.

"Is she…all right?" Ms. Blainey collapsed against a porch rail, gasping from her race to the house.

Cameron ignored her question and pressed a hand to Jennie's throat, searching for a pulse. Several long seconds passed before he felt the steady rhythm of blood circulating through her carotid artery.

Until that moment, he hadn't let the full impact hit him. Staring out over the yard toward the flaming structure in the distance, Cameron's chest tightened. The roof of the barn shuddered and then collapsed, sending a flurry of sparks into the air and fresh fuel into the fire. Flames licked the sky as the walls of the structure crumpled inward.

As he watched, the thought that Jennie had been in there roiled through his mind like a message on continuous replay. Cameron's stomach clenched and bile rose in his throat. If he hadn't gotten there in time…

"Lady?" Jennie struggled to sit up, coughing and hacking, her face covered in a thick layer of black soot. "Where's Lady?"

With a hand against her shoulder, Cameron held her down. "Relax, sweetheart. The horse made it out just fine."

Ms. Blainey's shaky laugh had an almost hysterical quality. "She almost dies in the fire and she's more worried about her horse."

"That's my Jennie." Cameron smoothed the sooty hair from her forehead.

She reached up and captured his fingers, her grip tight for all that she was weak. "I didn't see him until too late." In normal circumstances Jennie's voice was low and gravelly, like a sexy cat's purr. Her words now came out as though they'd been scraped over sandpaper. She clapped a hand to her mouth and coughed, her shoulders rolling and shaking with the force.

When the fit passed and she lay back, Cameron asked, "Him?"

"He hit me in the back of the head. By the time I came to my senses, he'd jammed the front door, tossed flames at the hay and ran out the back." Her eyes squeezed shut for a moment. "I swear I heard the sound of horse's hooves."

Fear for her clutched at his chest and Cameron gripped her forearms. "Someone did this on purpose?"

Her nod was almost imperceptible, but it reaffirmed the nightmare.

"Any idea who? Did you see his face?"

She shook her head and winced, a hand going up to the knot forming at the base of her skull. "Too dark. I tried to get out."

Ms. Blainey scurried toward the door. "I'll check on that ambulance."

"What the hell's going on out there?" Hank Ward's surly voice carried from the living room through the open doorway. "Why do I smell smoke? Where the hell did everyone go? Rachel? Jennie? Will someone answer?"

"He's not going to be happy." Rachel cast a look back at Jennie and Cameron before she ducked in. "Keep your shirt on, Hank Ward." She hurried inside.

Finally alone with Jennie, Cameron's guard slipped and a tremor shook him from head to toe. He reached out and pulled Jennie into his arms. "God, when I saw that fire and heard your voice inside the barn…" He buried his face in her hair, inhaling the acrid scent of smoke, grounding himself in the wonder of her physical reality after nearly losing her.

A long time had passed since he'd held her in his arms.

His hand caressed the side of her face and smoothed the soot-laden locks from her forehead. "Jesus, Jennie, you could have died."

"But I didn't." Her fingers knotted in his shirt and she pulled him closer, pressing her face against his shirt.

"I should have been here."

"You can't be everywhere," Jennie croaked. "I didn't do like you said and stay in the house. It was my fault."

She could stay forever in the circle of his arms, he wouldn't mind in the least. Then a cough racked her lungs and Cameron backed away, giving her room to force the ash and soot from her chest.

After a minute of coughing, she collapsed back against his arms, her eyes closed. "I need to sit up."

"You might have a concussion. Are you sure you should sit up?"

"Yes. I can breathe better that way."

He helped her to her feet. When she wobbled, he swooped her legs out from under her, carrying her to the porch swing.

As he settled her onto the cushioned seat, three horses burst over the top of the closest hill, racing toward the fire.

Jennie leaned forward, attempting to stand. "That'll be the guys. I need to help them put the fire out." The effort of those few words had her doubled over coughing once again.

"Like hell. You're suffering from a concussion and

smoke inhalation. The last thing you need is to be close to that fire." He pushed her back against the cushions. "As soon as Ms. Blainey comes out, I'll go help. You stay here until the ambulance arrives." He leaned across to peer into her face. "Are you going to be okay?"

Her eyes were bloodshot and rimmed with black, not her best look, but she was still beautiful to Cameron beneath the smudges of ash.

Jennie forced a smile. "I'm fine."

Cameron stood, a wry smile twisting his lips. "Sure."

Ms. Blainey stepped back through the doorway. "The emergency medical folks will be here in fifteen minutes." She smiled at Jennie. "They're sending the helicopter." In her hand, she carried a tall glass of iced water. "Thought you might need this."

Ms. Blainey's arrival was Cameron's cue to leave. If he stuck around, he might be tempted to kiss Jennie and he had no right to do that. Yet the urge was so powerful, Cameron hustled toward the stairs leading down and away from the house. He'd rather face a fiery blaze than his feelings for Jennie Ward.

JENNIE TOOK THE GLASS, her gaze following Cameron as he hurried down the steps and loped across the yard toward the barn.

Stan, Doug and Rudy were dragging water hoses toward the blaze, dampening the ground surrounding the huge fire.

Ms. Blainey cast a worried glance at the burning embers drifting toward the house. "Let's hope the wind doesn't pick up or we'll have a wildfire on our hands, as well."

Jennie watched, a headache raging as her strength

waned. She hated weakness, knowing she should be out there with the men battling the blaze. "There's no way they can put out that fire."

Rachel Blainey sat next to Jennie and pulled her against her shoulder. "Maybe not, but they'll keep it from spreading."

The enormity of the situation sank in and tears welled in Jennie's eyes. She dashed them away, refusing to cry in front of anyone. "What are we going to do? Every bit of our feed, hay and tack were in that barn."

"Don't you worry about it. We'll manage."

"You don't understand. We can't afford to replace any of it. If we have another hot dry summer like last year, we'll need hay to keep our horses and cattle alive through the winter." Her chest tightened at the thought of the Flying W being forced into bankruptcy. Another coughing fit racked her body. "We can't lose this ranch. It means everything to Dad. It'll kill him."

"You're dad is a tough guy. He'll manage just fine."

The whop-whop-whop sound of helicopter blades rose above the noise of the fire and the white-and-red emergency medical services helicopter appeared above the hilltops and landed out of sight on the opposite side of the big ranch house.

Jennie's throat hurt like a demon, but she had to warn Rachel. "Dad might be tough, but we have a ranch to run and someone's out to ruin us. Possibly kill us. Tell the helicopter to go back to the hospital, I can't leave Dad alone."

"He won't be alone." Cameron rounded the side of the house leading two paramedics carrying a stretcher between them.

She pressed her lips together, ready to do battle, but

another hacking cough rose in her throat and shook her until she lay against Rachel, limp and exhausted.

The paramedic climbed the steps and held an oxygen mask out in front of Jennie's face.

She pushed it aside, suppressing the next cough rising in her throat. "If I leave, he's on his own. How do I know someone won't torch the house or come in and shoot him?"

"One of the Prescott Personal Securities agents arrived at the Morgan Ranch a few minutes ago. I'll have him come keep an eye on your father while we're gone. He should be here before the helicopter takes off."

The cough forced its way out and Jennie doubled over, her throat aching from the heated air and smoke she'd breathed. Even the insides of her nostrils hurt.

"Ma'am, you really should wear this mask. It'll help you breathe easier." The paramedic lifted her wrist and checked her pulse.

"I'm not going," she choked out between bouts of coughing. Then she grabbed the oxygen mask from the paramedic and slapped it over her face. She frowned over the top of it at Cameron and muttered through the mask, "I'm not."

Cameron crossed his arms over his chest the way he used to when he wasn't getting his way, and he was settling in for the argument. "You could have a concussion and your throat could swell and close up. You're going."

The screen door opened and a voice chimed in. "Cameron's right. You're going to the hospital."

Jennie spun around to see her father's ashen face staring at her. He leaned heavily on a pair of crutches, the lines deeper around his mouth.

Ms. Blainey rushed forward. "You shouldn't be up, the doctor said to keep off that ankle for a week. No weight whatsoever or it won't heal properly."

"Stop fussing, woman. I needed to see to my daughter and find out what the heck was going on." His gaze moved toward what was left of the barn. The flames had died down as the fire ran out of fuel. Not much was left of the big old barn. Her father's Adam's apple bobbed several times and his gaze returned to Jennie. "Please, Jennie, go to the hospital. I'd feel much better knowing you were being taken care of."

She could only imagine the pain her father felt at seeing a barn his grandfather built now nothing but a pile of smoking rubble. Her father had been in and out of that barn for the past fifty-eight years. Memories of his father, his grandfather and his wife had to be swirling around in his head.

Jennie's heart ached for the man. "I'm sorry, Dad. I tried to put out the fire, but it was started in the hay."

Hank frowned down at her. "You think I care about that old barn? I couldn't give a damn about that old pile of rotting boards." His frown eased into a sad look. "I could have lost you. That's what I care about. We can rebuild a barn." He didn't say it, but his face said it all.

Jennie knew how much her father loved her mother and how much he loved her, his only daughter. He'd already lost one person he loved beyond reason. Of all people, Hank Ward knew better than most *you can rebuild a barn but you can't breathe life back into a dead person.*

Chapter Six

Cameron would have ridden to the hospital in the helicopter had there been room. Instead he saw Jennie safely onto the stretcher and loaded aboard the aircraft, promising he'd be there as soon as possible. After the helicopter was airborne, he retrieved his cell phone from his truck and stepped up on to the deck of the ranch house to watch the aircraft disappear over the treetops. At the same time, he dialed the Prescott Personal Securities agency.

Angel answered the phone. "PPS. You need a bodyguard, we got one for you. How can I help you?" The distinct sound of gum smacking clicked in Cameron's ear.

"Angel, this is Cameron Morgan, get me Mrs. Prescott." He held his breath, hoping beyond hope, Angel could manage this one request.

"She's in a meeting, Cam. Want me to take a message?"

The air he'd been holding shot out of his lungs as anger surged. "Get her, now."

"But—"

"Just do it." Jennie was flying through the air to Denver without his protection. Would whoever was trying to kill her be waiting at the hospital to finish the job? Worry ate away at his patience.

"Geez, you don't have to bite my head off."

Cameron wished he could reach through the phone and shake Angel. Why Evangeline picked up aggravating "strays," he couldn't begin to guess. She must have seen something redeemable in Angel, and for that, Cameron would give his boss the benefit of the doubt. "Please get Evangeline. It's very important."

"You could have said that in the first place. Hold on to your briefs, I'll ring her." The line went dead.

"Having problems with the receptionist?" Jack Sanders stepped out on the porch carrying a glass of lemonade, a grin curving his lips.

Cameron snorted. "She cut me off."

"Kinda like your brother did me, only he did it in person."

Hitting Redial, Cameron met Jack's clear, blue gaze. "How'd that go?"

Jack's snort echoed Cameron's. "You and your brother having some kind of sibling rivalry going on?"

Cameron pressed the receiver to his ear, his lips twisting. "Logan's had a bug up his butt since I started seeing Jennie twelve years ago. It only got worse when I left to join the army. What did he say?"

"It wasn't so much what he said, but how he said it." Jack shook his head. "The man stood in front of me holding a rifle like he knew what to do with it and wasn't afraid of using it on what he called a trespasser."

"Just like Logan to make a big show of it."

"A twelve-year-old grudge, huh?" Jack shoved a hand through his light brown hair. "Gotta be a statute of limitations on that."

"Tell me about it. The thirty-year-old grudge between the Wards and the Morgans tops that by a long shot."

"What started it?"

As Cameron shrugged, Angel's voice came on the line. "PPS. You need a bodyguard, we got one for you. How can I help you?"

"It's me again." Cameron ground his teeth to keep from yelling at the inept receptionist. "Could you please get Evangeline on the line?"

"She's right here. You shouldn't have hung up."

"I didn't."

"Cameron?" Evangeline's smooth tones eased a little of the tension from Cameron's shoulders. "What's happening?"

"We've had a couple attempts on the Ward family. Jennie's on the way to the hospital via AIRLIFE and Hank's laid up with a badly sprained ankle after someone took a potshot at him."

"Damn." Evangeline had never cursed to Cameron's knowledge. "Is Jennie going to be okay?"

"I hope so."

"How extensive are her injuries?"

His hand tightened on the phone. "Concussion and smoke inhalation."

"Smoke? What's going on out there?"

Cameron gave her the abbreviated version and ended with, "Could you get someone to the hospital to protect her at least until I can get there?"

"What about her father?"

Cameron shot a glance at his friend, the man he'd trusted with his own life on more than one operation in the Army Special Forces. "Jack's here."

"Huh." Her grunt of disapproval sounded through

the receiver. "Wasn't he supposed to go to your family?"

"They weren't very…hospitable."

"After what's happened to the Wards, I'm equally worried about them."

"They can take care of themselves until I can get Jennie back to the Flying W and Jack can go back to the Bar M. I'll work something out with my mother and sister to make sure Jack gets in." Even if his father and brother refused help, that was no excuse for denying his mother and younger sister some form of added protection.

Cameron fought a deep, burning anger that raged beneath the surface, coursing through every fiber of his being. While he'd been out banging his head against a wall with his father and brother, someone had gone after Jennie. He needed to find who'd tried to kill her and take him out—preferably limb by limb.

First, he had to make sure Jennie was all right. "I don't like leaving Jennie without protection for too long. I'm on my way to the hospital in my truck, ETA forty-five minutes. Jack will be here with Hank."

"I'll take care of providing protection for Jennie. Shouldn't you stay put and see what you can find out about who might have hit her and burned the barn?"

Cameron's hand clenched around the thin cell phone. Jennie would be in a big hospital in the mile-high city of Denver. They had no idea who'd tried to kill her. Could he stay back at the Flying W knowing she could be in danger?

Hell no.

"I have to go." His voice was firm, unrelenting.

"Are you sure you're the right man for this job? I

worried from the beginning that you might not be able to distance yourself. Are you still carrying a torch for Jennie Ward?"

Was he? The knife to the gut at hearing her voice through the door of a burning barn should have been a big enough clue. Was he hung up on Jennie? Had he ever not been hung up on her?

"We can talk about it later. I'm headed to Denver." He clicked the end button and pocketed the cell phone.

"Evangeline's not too happy about how close you are to the Ward woman." Jack shook his cup, his gaze on the ice swirling around in the lemonade. "She wanted me to come out and trade places with you."

"I can handle this."

"And keep a clear head?" Jack gave him a look that indicated his skepticism. "I know if Kelly were in as much danger, I wouldn't be thinking too straight. Then again, I'd want to be the one protecting her." He held up his hands. "Not that I wouldn't trust someone like you, but I couldn't live with myself if she got hurt."

"Exactly. No matter how I feel about Jennie, I can't let someone else provide her protection. I'd be completely useless wondering what was happening to her."

Jack smiled. "Sounds like you still have a thing for her."

"Maybe I do, maybe I don't." He wasn't ready to admit to anything. "She's like family. I can't turn my back on her."

"Do you feel the same way about your own family?"

"Of course. Jennie's like my little sister, Molly." Cameron turned away to hide the lie in his eyes. "She's like a sister." Like hell. He yearned to do certain unbrotherly things with Jennie. She melted his insides like ice cream on hot pavement. The thought of her dying in the smoke-filled barn twisted his gut into a tight wad.

The sooner he got to her, the better. "I have to go."

"Don't worry about anything here. I'll keep a close watch on Mr. Ward."

Cameron stared hard at his friend. "Stay alert."

Jack tipped a finger off his brow. "Roger that."

JENNIE SWAM in and out of consciousness throughout the evening and into the night. A strange man showed up at her door claiming he was from Prescott Personal Securities and he would be her bodyguard for the night. A call from Cameron confirmed.

With a scratchy throat, a headache the size of Texas and a sense of gloom and doom creeping in around her, she sank into a blue funk not at all helped by the mild sedative prescribed by the doctor.

Deep down she'd hoped Cameron would show up at the hospital. And what? Hold her hand through the night like a worried lover? *Dream on, girl.*

Her dreams were anything but restful. Smoke clouded her vision and a monster lurked in the swirling shadows, ready to pounce on her and leave her to burn. Tossing and turning, she fell into a restless sleep, until ten after eight the next morning.

Morning light shone through the window, warming her blankets and urging her eyes to open. The acrid scent of disinfectant reminded Jennie she wasn't in her bed at home. Turning her head to the side, she rolled over on the goose egg caused by the man who'd hit her in the barn. "Ouch." The sound came out as a croak and she reached up to test the sore spot.

"So you finally decided to wake up?" Cameron's

low, smooth voice brought her the rest of the way awake, alerting her senses to the sounds of the nurses delivering breakfast trays to patients up and down the hallway. He sat in the chair beside her bed, his hair mussed as if he'd slept there, one lock falling over his forehead.

Just seeing him there made the gloom of the night before dissipate. Jennie's world brightened and she felt better already, even though she shouldn't let Cameron's presence have that effect on her. Given all that had happened, she didn't fight it for now. Later. She'd fight her feelings later. After breakfast.

The scent of eggs and toast drifted through the open doorway and her stomach made a loud grumbling sound. Heat flooded her cheeks and she pressed a hand to her belly.

Cameron smiled. "Hungry?"

"I guess I didn't get around to dinner last night." Her words rumbled from her chest all gravelly and hoarse, but her throat wasn't as tight as it had been the night before. "Think I could get something easy to swallow?"

"Coming right up." Cameron rose and pulled over a tray loaded with a covered plate, a carton of juice and plastic utensils. He lifted the cover to display an array of scrambled eggs and oatmeal. Nothing with a hard edge to force down her battered throat. Even hospital food looked good to her right now.

Jennie tucked into the scrambled eggs, fighting to swallow every last bite. Working the ranch, she never had to worry about calories and ate with gusto. Halfway through the meal, the effort was too much and she pushed the tray aside, happy with what she'd managed.

A worried frown creased Cameron's forehead. "How's the throat?"

"Not so great, but I'll live." She could put up with a lot to know she'd be around another day to help her father. Speaking of which… Jennie glanced around the room. "I don't suppose anyone's brought me some clean clothes?"

Cameron lifted an overnight bag from the floor next to him and laid it across her bed. "I had Ms. Blainey pack a few things for you."

She rifled through noting the jeans, blouse, clean underwear and toothbrush.

"The nurse said the doctor makes his rounds around ten. They won't release you until he gives the okay."

"Ten?" Her hands paused in their search through her belongings and her brows drew together. She didn't like hospitals and didn't intend to stay any longer than she had to. "I feel fine."

"Hang tough, Jenn. Ten is not that long to wait."

A tingle shivered across her skin from the way he shortened her name as he had when they'd dated so many years ago. "What about Dad? He's out on the ranch by himself."

"Another bodyguard from PPS, Jack Sanders, is there. He'll make sure your dad is taken care of."

She pushed her hair back from her face and grimaced at the tangled mess. "I don't suppose there's a brush in here." The nurses had allowed her to shower the soot and grime away from her skin before she had climbed into the hospital gown and between the snowy, white sheets. She hadn't had access to a comb or brush to pull through the tangles, settling for a brief finger-combing through her hair. Since she'd slept restlessly, it was a tangled mess. Feeling around inside the bag again, she located her favorite brush and sighed. After several attempts at pulling the tangles free, she rested her arm. "I could have used conditioner last night."

"Here, let me." Cameron relieved her of the brush and sat beside her on the bed. Taking one length of hair at a time in his long calloused fingers, he eased the tangles free.

His leather and aftershave scent teased Jennie's senses. "Hey, you're good." She relaxed and enjoyed the feeling of his hands smoothing across her scalp and through her hair.

"I used to do this for Molly when she was little. Mom was always dealing with other things and didn't have time to take it easy. But don't tell anyone. It doesn't fit the tough-guy image."

"My lips are sealed." She practically purred at the way he was making her feel. When he had the brush gliding smoothly through her hair, the relaxed feeling changed and her body tensed. Having Cameron comb her hair felt too intimate. Too sensual. The only thing between her and him was one very thin hospital gown, with the back gaping wide….

Jennie gasped and jerked to the side and away from Cameron. With her face burning, she hoped he hadn't noticed her back had been naked for him see.

Cameron stood, a smile quirking up the side of his face. "Uh, you might want to close the nightgown a bit before you get out of bed."

"Oh, you!" Jennie grabbed the brush and would have hit him with it, if he hadn't moved out of reach.

"Temper, temper. I was only trying to save you the effort."

"Yeah, right." Her anger faded as she recalled all he'd done for her in the past twenty-four hours. "Cameron, about yesterday…thanks."

His smile disappeared. "Don't thank me. I wasn't there when you needed me."

"Yes, you were." Her gaze locked with his. "If you hadn't come when you did, I'd have died in that barn."

"If I hadn't left to go to the Bar M, perhaps the barn would never have burned."

"Or maybe it would have with both of us in it."

"Which brings us back to who hit you and set the fire."

Jennie's shoulders slumped. "All I saw was a shadowy figure running past me to the door. I was too worried about the lighted matchbook to look at the back of his head when he opened the door." She scrunched her eyes closed. "But I did hear the sound of a horse's hooves. Whoever torched the barn was on horseback."

"Have you seen any strangers around the ranch, lately?"

"No. It's just me, Dad and the hands."

"What about in Dry Wash?"

The question was reasonable. Dry Wash was small enough everyone knew everyone else. If a new person moved to town or showed up in the bars, people would talk about it for days. But Jennie had been working the ranch every day. She'd left all the shopping to Ms. Blainey. The last time she'd been in Dry Wash was to fill her truck with diesel. "I don't know." Was her life so filled with ranch work, she'd forgotten how to have a life? The thought didn't sit well with her. Especially knowing Cameron had been out in the world, exploring new places and meeting people.

Jennie reminded herself, this was her choice. Her father couldn't run the ranch on his own. He needed his family and that consisted of one daughter. Her.

"After the snake in the feed bin and the razor blade in your saddle, did you see any signs of someone having been there, something being out of place?"

She shook her head. "Nothing. The hands usually stay in the bunkhouse, except for an occasional visit to family or a late-night poker game in town. The night before the razor incident, they'd all gone into Dry Wash to see Jimmy D and his band play at the Rustler Saloon. The only folks there were me, Dad and Ms. Blainey. Anyone could have sneaked into the barn and planted that razor. Up until then, we saw no need to put locks on the barn doors. No one bothered anything."

Until recently.

The sound of voices in the hall pulled Jennie's attention away from Cameron in time to see Sheriff Hodges from Dry Walsh push through the doorway.

The frown on his face made Jennie's stomach churn the scrambled eggs she'd eaten. She'd known Sheriff Hodges all her life. He normally smiled and joked with the folks of the county, saving his frown for those who broke the law.

He nodded to Cameron and his frowning gaze rested on Jennie. "The fire inspector got to work early this morning."

"I can tell him how the fire was started," Jennie said. "The man who hit me in the head dropped a pack of lit matches in the hay."

The sheriff nodded and broke eye contact to stare down at the uniform cowboy hat in his hands. "They found remnants of the matchbook all right, and something else." He glanced up, his eyes darting from Cameron back to Jennie. "They found a body."

Chapter Seven

Jennie's face blanched. "A body? Whose body? Oh my God. Stan, Rudy, Doug—where are they?"

Cameron held up his hand. Jennie didn't need to get all excited after everything she'd already been through. "Whoa. Calm down. The three hands showed up before the helicopter landed at the ranch yesterday evening. They helped to keep the fire from spreading."

Jennie shook her head. "Who else could it be?"

The sheriff tapped his hat to his thigh. "I was hoping you could tell us."

"Me?" Jennie's face tipped to the side, her brows drawn together. "I thought there was only one man in the barn—the one who hit me in the back of the head and ran out the back door."

"According to the fire inspector, there was another next to the hay stack." The sheriff pulled a small notepad from his pocket. "So you're telling me you didn't see the other man?"

"No, the lights weren't working. I know my way around without them. I didn't see anybody until I saw the guy who hit me out of the corner of my eye."

Sheriff Hodges flipped open the notepad. Then he

dug around the same pocket for a pen. "Can you describe that man?"

"No, like I said, it was dark and I only saw him from the corner of my eye. More like a shadow. Then he hit me." She told the sheriff about playing dead until the man ran out the back door leaving his gift of fire.

The image of smoke pouring from the roof of the barn and Jennie's voice calling out from inside left Cameron's belly hollow. He ran his hand across the bristles on his chin, the sleepless night weighing heavily on his mental capacity. "Look, Sheriff, as you know there have been several attempts on Hank and Jennie Ward's lives in the past couple days with the razor blade, snake and shooting incidents. Before that fences were cut and cattle had gone missing. Perhaps there were two men involved, one of which is now dead in the barn."

The sheriff nodded. "We'll consider that. In the meantime, we've sent what's left of the body to the medical examiner. Don't go too far from home, Miss Ward. We may have more questions for you."

"For me?" Jennie stared up at him. "Why me?"

"You were the only other person in the barn that we can verify."

Her brows wrinkled over her forehead. "But what about the other man?"

"We're checking into the evidence. The state crime lab will be involved as well now that there's been a death." He glanced from Jennie to Cameron. "A detective from the Colorado Bureau of Investigations Major Crime Unit will be by to question you about the fire." He nodded and left the room.

Stunned silence followed the sheriff's departure.

"Why do I get the really bad feeling I'm a suspect in all this? I'm the victim here, not the other way around." Jennie flung the sheet aside and stood. "I'll be damned if I sit back and take this."

Cameron couldn't help the smile curving his lips. Jennie Ward madder than hell and dressed in a wispy, thin hospital nightgown was a welcome sight to see. "What do you plan to do? I don't suggest you go running out of the hospital like that." He nodded at her attire.

Jennie glanced down at her gown and back up to Cameron as if he hadn't said anything. "Who the hell was in that barn besides me? And I mean both alive and dead."

"Let the coroner do his job for the answer to the dead guy question. As for the live one, we could try to follow where the hoof prints lead."

Jennie shook her head. "As dry as it's been, there won't be a lot of tracks. Not to mention, we have a ranch full of tracks from our own horses and cattle scattered all over the Flying W."

A tentative knock sounded on the door and Cameron's mother poked her head around the side. "Oh good, Cameron, I'm glad you're here." She stepped through the door wearing a clean pair of jeans, a light blue blouse and carrying an overflowing vase of gerbera daisies. "How are you, Jennie?" The older woman kissed Cameron on the cheek and glanced at Jennie, an open, friendly smile on her face. "I'm so glad to see you up and about. What a scare we all had about the fire. Want me to put these on the night table?"

"Thank you." Jennie smiled, tentatively.

"Oh, pardon me, we haven't been formally introduced. I'm Emma Morgan. Cameron's mother."

"I know who you are, I just…"

"Wondered what I was doing here?" His mother's smile made Cameron glad she was the person she was—open, honest and friendly. "I know, I've been remiss in paying my respects to my neighbors, but I'll be damned if I let my husband's and your father's silliness interfere in what's right a moment longer. We should have known each other for all the years you've been alive." Emma Morgan's stern look melted into a grin. "Sorry. I get a little riled at times. I wasn't raised with great manners, like your mother."

Jennie tugged at her gown in an attempt to close the gap in back and eased toward the bed. "You knew my mother?"

"Oh yes. At one time, we were all friends. But that's an old story and I don't want to bore you with it."

As JENNIE SCOOTED beneath the bedsheets, Cameron pulled out a chair and set it in front of his mother. "Bore us, Mother. It's about time." For years, he'd bugged his mother to tell him why there were bad feelings between the two families.

"There's not much to the story, really. It all happened so long ago it seems silly…" Cameron's mother twisted a string hanging on to the edge of a sheet, her happy face of a few moments before clouded.

Cameron wanted to shake his father for putting that shadow in his mother's eyes. Whatever the problem, they could have worked it out for all parties concerned.

Jennie reached out and grasped the woman's hand. "You don't have to tell us anything, if you don't want."

"Don't tell her that." Cameron scooted a chair beside his mother and perched on the edge. "I've been asking for years. If she says she wants to tell her story, by all means, let her."

His mother rolled her eyes. "You're right, I should have told you a long time ago. I just didn't feel it was my right, and I guess I was a bit embarrassed."

Jennie stared at Cameron's mother, her eyes widened. "Embarrassed?"

"I know, I shouldn't be, but there you have it." She shrugged. "Hank, Tom, Louise and I all went to high school together. I guess you could say Hank, Tom and I were friends before Louise entered the picture. I was a tomboy even back then."

"Big surprise." Cameron reached across and squeezed his mother's hand. "I think that's part of your charm."

"Because you're my son." She smiled at him and pulled her hand free. "Tom and Hank only ever saw me as one of the guys because I could ride, rope and shoot as good as or better than them. Then they discovered Louise." Emma Morgan gave Jennie a sad smile.

"My mother."

"Yes. And she was the most beautiful and elegant girl in the school. She always knew what to wear, how to wear it and what shoes went best with it. Before Louise, I fit in. After Tom and Hank discovered Louise, I might as well have been invisible." Her gaze shifted to the window as if gazing at a picture of her past.

Cameron's heart squeezed for the young woman ignored by her two best friends.

"Louise started dating Tom first. But Hank and Tom were always together. It was bound to happen. I don't know why they didn't see it coming." Emma Morgan chuckled and stared down at her hands.

"They both fell in love with Louise?" Jennie asked.

Emma emitted a soft snort. "Boy, did they."

"So that's what caused the feud?" Cameron jumped ahead. "Hank married Louise and Tom was jealous?" A flash of anger skidded through him. Had his father been a bigger jackass than he thought?

"Don't go being ugly to your father." His mother patted his hand. "When Louise told Hank she'd marry him, Tom took it pretty well on the surface. He wished his friend Hank the best."

"But?" Jennie prompted.

"I think Tom felt like Hank stole the beautiful Louise from him. Then he asked me to marry him. Looking back, I realize it was on the rebound. I think subconsciously, I knew that, but I married him anyway because I'd fallen in love with the big guy.

"We were all still friends, although the relationship was a little strained. After a particularly bad argument between Tom and myself, I went to the only friend I had for a shoulder to cry on."

"Hank," Cameron supplied.

His mother nodded. "Hank met me at the diner in Dry Wash, and I cried on his shoulder. He told me to go back home and work things out. When I got up to leave, he hugged me and told me he loved me. I knew it was like a friend, maybe even a sister." Emma stared up into Cameron's eyes. "Your father came looking for me about that time and saw the hug and heard Hank tell me he loved me."

Cameron shook his head. "And I'm sure Dad stuck around for the explanation." His father was as hot-tempered as they come and jumped to conclusions too often to count.

"No. He didn't bother to hear me out. He punched Hank in the nose and told him to stay away from the Bar M or he'd shoot him."

"All over a misunderstanding?" Jennie asked.

"That's right, and a healthy dose of pigheadedness. I suppose Tom thought Hank stole Louise from him and was working on taking me away, as well. I should have been flattered, but I was mad about him hitting Hank. Tom and I didn't talk for weeks. Then I found out I was pregnant." She gave a bark of mirthless laughter. "Tom finally figured out he'd better make me happy or I'd leave, but he never backed off on his decree to Hank."

"Were you ever afraid Tom still loved my mother?" As soon as she spoke the question, Jennie clapped a hand to her mouth. "I'm sorry. I shouldn't have asked that."

Cameron silently agreed, but at the same time, this was the most his mother had ever opened up about the rift or anything else about her relationship with his father. He wanted to know, too. "Were you?"

She smiled at Cameron, a smile that didn't reach her eyes. "I couldn't help feeling that way. Tom was so mad when Louise chose Hank, it took him a couple weeks back then before he would talk to either of them. When he asked me to marry him, I knew I was his second choice."

"Didn't that bother you?" Jennie asked.

"Not really. I knew what I was getting into. You see, I've loved Tom since I was old enough to know the difference between boys and girls. He just never saw me until Hank married Louise. I thought he'd learn to love me, eventually."

Cameron thought back over the years. His father had never been openly affectionate with his mother, nor had he been with his children. He'd always thought it was because his father wasn't demonstrative.

His mother frowned at him. "Now, don't go thinking your father doesn't really love me or his children, because he does. He's never been one to show it openly. I think that might have been part of the reason why Louise finally decided to marry Hank." She grabbed his hand and squeezed. "Your father loves you, too."

Cameron's chest tightened. After ten years of silence, he'd given up on his father. "He has a funny way of showing it."

"I think he felt betrayed, and was doing his pig-headed thing when you started dating Jennie." Her other hand reached out to grab Jennie's. "I had hoped your relationship would bring the two families back together."

Cameron had hoped for that, as well, but it didn't. The chasm between him and his father grew the longer he saw Jennie.

"That you didn't want to stay and work the ranch like his father before him broke his heart." His mother sighed and dropped their hands. "A more stubborn man, I've never met and your brother is turning out just like him."

"What's wrong with Logan?" Jennie's gaze shifted to Cameron.

"Nothing."

"He's taken on his father's grudge with a vengeance." Cameron's mother inhaled deeply and let it out. "No matter what I say, he won't listen to reason. It's as if he likes being miserable."

"And I thought my dad was a lost cause." Jennie smiled at the older woman. "Despite the ongoing feud, Molly and I have been friends. I met her at the county fair when she was little. Even at ten, she could ride a barrel horse like nobody's business."

"That's Molly." Cameron's mother beamed.

Cameron stood. "Thanks, Mom, for letting us know about what started all this."

His mother rose and slipped her plain, leather purse over her shoulder. "Well, I have some shopping to do while I'm in Denver. I need a new bridle for Topper and a couple new girths."

A smile curved Cameron's lips. "That's my mother, she'd rather shop for her horses than for a new pair of shoes like most women."

"That was always the difference between me and your mother." Emma Morgan stood and patted Jennie's hand. "You look just like her."

"Sadly, that's where the likeness stops." Though Jennie was looking at Emma Morgan, her golden eyes appeared glazed over with the past. "I've never been a girlie girl, even when my mother was alive. She tried, but I wasn't having any of it. I'd rather be riding horses than shopping. I'd be like a fish out of water."

"You and me both." Cameron's mother faced him with a stern look. "Take good care of this girl, son."

"I'll do my best." Cameron walked with his mother to the door. "You be careful, too. You shouldn't be in Denver on your own."

"I'm not. Logan brought me."

A familiar tug pulled at Cameron's gut. What had gone so wrong between him and his brother that they were like strangers?

Emma waved at Jennie, her smile looking more forced. "Take care of yourself, honey."

"I will," Jennie's voice ground out in a hoarse whisper.

The door closed behind his mother and Cameron stared at the solid wood separating him from his family.

"If there's one thing I've learned in my life…" Jennie started, and then paused.

Cameron turned to face her. "What have you learned?"

"When the going gets tough, family's all you've got."

Her statement hit him square in the chest. "I'll be right back." Cameron left without looking back, his mind on the woman in the hallway.

Cameron spied his mother several doors down. "Wait up, Mom."

His mother stopped and turned to him her brows raised. "Did I forget something?"

"No, I wanted to ask you something without involving Jennie."

"Okay, shoot." She stood with her hands on her hips, the straight-talking country girl he'd grown up loving and respecting for her strength and courage.

"What do you know about Brad, your new ranch hand?"

"Only that he's well-mannered and good with the horses. We hired him on when Ty broke his leg."

"That's about all Molly could tell me, as well."

"You know your father, he likes to go on his gut feel when hiring. I stay out of the way unless I have a strong opinion one way or another. With Brad, I thought he was nice enough and he was good with the horses. Why do you ask?"

"With all that's going on, and him being new, keep an eye on him. You and Molly should stay close to each other—you know, safety in numbers and all."

"Do you think Brad might have had anything to do with the fire?"

"I don't know who started it, but whoever did it killed a man."

"What?" His mother placed a hand on Cameron's arm. "What man?"

He told her what the sheriff had told him and Jennie.

By the time he got to the end of the short version, his mother's face had paled and her head swayed from side to side. "Holy cow."

"No kidding." He gripped his mother's shoulders. "All the more reason for you and Molly to keep your eyes open. Trust no one. Jack will be over as soon as we get back to the Flying W. Make sure he isn't threatened at gunpoint this time, will you?"

His mother's lips twisted. "I'll have a word with Tom." She reached up and cupped his face with as much emotion as he'd ever seen her express in public. "Cameron, I love you."

"Same here, Mom." He hugged her to him and let go, anxious to return to Jennie.

Once his mother disappeared down the hallway, Cameron reentered the room, his mind on the Bar M and one new cowboy there. He'd been ready to ride when Cameron went into the barn to collect his saddle. Did that give the man enough time to ride over to the Flying W, kill someone and hit Jennie over the head? Maybe. Seemed a bit far-fetched, but he couldn't discount anyone with a horse. Which also meant he had to check out every one of the Flying W ranch hands. Jennie wouldn't be happy if she knew he had them on his list of suspects.

Chapter Eight

Clouds cloaked the sun and sky, high enough for a clear view of the mountains but too high for relief from the late-spring dry spell. If they didn't get rain soon, they wouldn't have enough hay to feed the horses and cattle through the winter. Having been through hard times over the past year, the Flying W was already on the edge financially. With the loss of the barn and the probability of a skimpy hay crop, they'd have to sell cattle while the market was low. As a last resort they'd have to sell acreage that had been in their family for a century. As far as Jennie was concerned, selling was not an option.

As the truck entered the yard and swung around to the side entrance of the Ward ranch house, Jennie forced herself to stare at the mass of ash and charred timbers where the Wards had raised horses for the past hundred years. She tried not to dwell on the loss. She also tried not to think about how glad she was that Cameron had been there to save her or that he was the one to deliver her home from the hospital. If his presence helped her to keep herself together, she wouldn't place any importance on it. Deep in her heart she had to admit, she didn't know how she'd be holding up without Cameron by her side, nor did she want to try.

Cameron reached out and laid his hand over hers. "It can be rebuilt."

An unexpected thrill of hope flickered through her and Jennie had to remind herself Cameron was only talking about the barn, not any future they might have together. "I know." Her voice caught in her sore throat. Was it the sore throat or the tears threatening every mile closer they'd got to the disaster? "It'll be all shiny and new with none of the memories or character of the old barn. My dad must be beside himself." *She* was.

"I'm sure he was just glad to know his only daughter didn't die in the fire. Anything else can be dealt with. Losing a family member...not so easy."

"Yeah." Memories of her mother's death surfaced to combine with the loss of the barn. Louise Ward had been buried on just such a day—in the late spring with a pall of clouds hanging over the mountaintops.

As Cameron helped Jennie from the truck, Jack Sanders stepped out of the house onto the porch and leaned against a column. "Glad you're back."

Jennie glanced up at the man and noted the strain around her mouth. "Is my father giving you fits?"

Jack gave her a tight smile. "You could say that. He's very frustrated he can't do anything about the mess outside. More than once, Ms. Blainey and I caught him making his way by crutches to the door. If he's not careful, that ankle isn't the only thing he'll have to worry about."

Jennie ignored the last remark, fixing on what she could do something about. "His ankle will never get better if he doesn't give it a rest." She lifted the plastic hospital bag filled with her sooty clothing from the floorboard of Cameron's truck and braced herself for a confrontation with her headstrong father.

ONCE JENNIE PASSED through the screen door and the springs slammed it shut, Jack turned to Cameron. "Ready for me to go to the Bar M?"

"Yeah, my mother's expecting you, and I'll call her to give her the heads-up you're on your way. She'll be there to guide you past any roadblocks you might encounter."

"Like your brother?"

Cameron's lips thinned. "Or my father."

"Great. I'm going in to protect a family from being targeted by an unknown threat and my life is at risk from the known." He smiled. "Seems we've been in similar situations on more than one occasion in the Special Forces."

Cameron's lips twisted. He found it sad to think his father and brother were considered dangerous to a man like Jack. "Consider it the threat of friendly fire."

Jack chuckled. "Or in this case, unfriendly fire." He stepped off the porch onto the parched ground. "Guess I better get over there."

"One other thing." Cameron checked to make sure Jennie wasn't around before he added, "Find out what you can about the new ranch hand, Bradley Carter."

Jack's eyes widened. "Think he's our guy?"

"I don't know, but it's as good a place as any to start."

"I'll do that. I'll also put a call into PPS on my way over and have Lenny run a background check on him."

"Good. I'll run a check on the other ranch hands here

at the Flying W." He stared at the burned-out barn. "After what happened yesterday, I don't trust anyone."

"I'll let you know what I find out."

As Cameron entered the house, the sound of raised voices led him to the living room.

"There's nothing wrong with me I can't handle on a pair of crutches. I refuse to have women mollycoddling me when I have a ranch to run." Hank Ward struggled to get out of his recliner without the aid of crutches. "Give me those dadgum crutches!"

"Get over it, Hank Ward. You're not getting them." Ms. Blainey set a tray of coffee on the table beside his recliner. "The doctor said if you don't want to walk with a permanent limp, you have to stay off that ankle for at least a week, two would be better." She planted her hands on her hips and glared down at him. "You want to walk with a limp the rest of your life?"

"I need to see what can be salvaged," he blustered, refusing to answer her question.

"There's nothing left, Dad. The barn and all that was in it is a complete loss." Jennie's voice was flat and emotionless. If her eyes were a bit glazed, her father didn't seem to notice.

Cameron did. Had she been any other woman but Jennie Ward, she'd have broken down by now. Not his Jennie.

He shook his head. Why was he even considering her his Jennie? She hadn't been his since they were in school together. She probably wouldn't have him after he'd forced her to make the choice to leave with him or stay with her father. Had her father and the Flying W been out of the equation, Cameron knew she'd have gone with him.

Being an only child, Jennie's sense of family and duty was as deeply engrained as the Morgan's. Cameron's departure from the Bar M had been a blow to his father. Cameron had reasoned that his brother, Logan, was there to carry on the Morgan legacy and help his father raise the cattle and horses. Even Molly talked about coming back to the ranch or at least Dry Wash after college and veterinary school to set up a veterinarian practice close by. The ranch was in their blood.

So what had happened to Cameron's rancher gene? He stared out the living room windows with their view of the east range of the Rockies and sighed. Maybe he'd stayed away so long because he knew if he came back he might be reminded of how much he missed the ranch, working with his hands, getting rough and dirty.

Jennie's father turned his anger and frustration on Cameron. "You're the bodyguard. What are you doing about making sure someone doesn't take another shot at killing my daughter?" He gave Cameron a full-length appraisal. "You don't even carry a gun. How are you supposed to keep her safe without a gun?"

"I have a brain. I don't need a gun to protect your daughter, sir." Cameron was used to this question. When he'd hired on to the PPS agency, he'd told Evangeline flat out he didn't want to carry a gun. Because of the tremor in his hands, he didn't trust his aim. He preferred to use his hands to settle arguments and he'd always managed to prevail even when his opponent was armed.

"Well a brain ain't necessarily going to stop someone from putting a bullet through my little girl."

"Guns aren't the answer to everything, sir."

"Maybe not, but I'd feel a sight better knowing you were carrying a gun."

"Leave him alone, Dad." Jennie stepped between him and her father. "He does things the way he wants, and he's good at it."

Cameron's chest swelled at her defense, at the same time he wanted to tell her to leave it. "I can handle this, Jennie." He could fight his own battles and had been doing so since he started walking. He and Logan had their share of fights as kids, rough-housing to the point they were banned from the house during the daylight hours.

"Maybe so, but I'm tired of the noise." Jennie gave her father a tough stare and scrubbed a hand through her hair. "I need a ride."

"After suffering a concussion and almost dying in a fire?" Ms. Blainey crossed her arms over her chest. "I don't think so."

Jennie cast a desperate look toward Cameron. "If I don't get outside soon, I'll go stir-crazy."

"Ha! Tell that to the housekeeper from hell!" Hank groused.

Cameron pointed a finger at Mr. Ward. "Stay inside and away from the windows."

The older man's eyes narrowed. "I don't take orders from a Morgan."

"Fine, then pin a target to your chest and walk on out to that barn you're so anxious to get to." Jennie threw her arms in the air and stalked toward the door. "I'm going for a ride."

"Aren't you forgetting something?" her father asked.

She stopped and slowly turned back. "What?"

"All the saddles burned up in the barn."

Her shoulders slumped to the point she looked like a bedraggled puppy freshly in from a cold rain. "Oh yeah."

Cameron made a mental note to call his sister and ask if they had a saddle to spare for Jennie. "Come on. We'll walk down by the pond."

"Right." Hank snorted. "Like that doesn't give every lunatic a chance to shoot a hole through her. I thought you had a brain."

"Enough!" Jennie grabbed Cameron's hand and tugged him toward the door. "I don't care if someone shoots me. It would be preferable to this man's lousy temper!"

Cameron cast a pointed look at Ms. Blainey. "Don't let him close to the windows or anywhere outside."

She nodded, her lips firm. "If I have to drug his coffee or give him a concussion, I'll keep him inside."

"Like hell, woman." Hank slammed his hand against the armrest of his chair, the jolt making him wince and ease his backside to the side.

Ms. Blainey walked with them to the door, dropping her tone to a whisper. "You two go on. He'll be fine. He's just a little cranky."

Jennie rolled her eyes. "A little?"

"Go." Rachel shooed them toward the door. "Stay close to the shadows and keep your head down."

Cameron chuckled. "You sound like my drill sergeant from basic. Ever been in the army dressed as a man?"

With a rosy blush, Ms. Blainey hurried back to Hank, leaving Cameron and Jennie alone for the first time since they'd arrived at the Flying W.

He stepped in front of her and opened the door,

glancing left to right before he let her out. "Like she said, keep low and stay close to the shadows."

JENNIE WANTED to shove Cameron off the porch for behaving like a commando on a mission. All she wanted was to get a breath of fresh, clean air that didn't smell like a hospital or a burned-out barn. She didn't want to attack a village in the jungle. Still, she kept close to the shadows and moved behind Cameron, letting him lead the way with his large frame. Not that someone couldn't shoot her from behind as easily as from the front.

As they moved toward the wooded area to the south of the stocked fishpond, Jennie let her gaze rove over Cameron's backside. His shoulders were broader than ten years ago, and back then they'd been pretty broad, what with his football and ranch chores bulking him out at an early age. "Any ideas about who that was in the barn with me?"

Cameron walked on a few steps farther before answering. "Not really."

"Either you do or you don't."

"I think we should look at everyone with access to the ranch by horse."

"That could be anyone."

"True, but we have to look at who has the most to gain from getting rid of you and your father."

"I thought you said there was oil on the land. Isn't that reason enough?" She hurried to catch up and walked with him side by side. "Who would have access to that information? Can't you follow that lead?"

"Unfortunately, that could be just about anyone. I'm betting the CEOs who invested in the Kingston Trust didn't know about the oil on their property. But someone did. Both were deep in debt for one reason or another, which forced them to sell." Cameron moved her to the side between him and the tree line.

"Do you think that's what this is all about? Someone is trying to force us out and since we haven't left yet, they'll kill us to get us off?"

"Yeah, that's my assumption."

"But who?"

"That's the sixty-four-million-dollar question." A twig crunched and Cameron swung in front of her so fast, she didn't have time to check her long strides and ran into his chest.

He reached out to steady her, his hands closing around her upper arms. A squirrel leaped from branch to branch in the trees beside them.

Jennie laughed at the animal scurrying away. "A bit punchy, are we?" All the laughter died when the warmth of his fingers spread throughout her body.

After Cameron dropped his hands, the heat ebbed, leaving behind a dull chill. She ached for the security his touch brought. A far cry from the way she'd responded to her husband's touch eight years ago. Had it really been eight years since Vance's death?

Cameron shoved his hands in his pockets as if to keep them off her. "I need to ask you some tough questions you may not like."

"Okay," she answered slowly, responding to the seriousness of his voice.

"Stan's been with the Flying W for a long time, hasn't he?"

"Since before I was born."

"What about the other two hands?"

Jennie backed away, her previous warm imaginings about this man evaporating like spilled water on bone-dry soil. "Why?"

"Have you ever had any issues with them?"

"No, never." She shook her head and stared at him. "Doug's been with us for ten years and Rudy ever since he graduated from high school over a year and a half ago." Her mind scrambled to grasp the direction his questions had taken. "You don't think they could have burned the barn down with a man inside, do you?"

He didn't answer, just stared at her.

Heat surged into her face. "Well, you're wrong. I'd trust them with my life."

"That might be well and good. Do you trust them with your father's life?"

The sharp retort poised on Jennie's lips dried up before she could snap it out. Would she trust Doug or Rudy with her father's life after last night? Before Cameron had questioned her, she would have answered yes. But now…

Anger spiked in her gut and swelled upward to consume her in a cataclysmic rage. "Damn you." She forced the words between clenched teeth.

"Why?" He reached for her, but she knocked his hands away.

"Damn you for inserting that little bit of doubt into my mind." She stomped away from him, heading toward the water. "Just go to hell, Cameron Morgan. I don't need you to play bodyguard for me or my father. You've been gone for ten years. Then you show up all holier-than-thou and start casting suspicion on my ranch hands." She turned and faced him, hands on her hips. "I won't have it. Why don't you go away like you did before? Run away from the life you were born to lead, from the family who loved you. Leave, because that's what you do best."

A sucker punch to the gut couldn't have been more painful. Cameron drew in a slow breath and let it out his nose like a prize bull ready to stampede. "I left because I dared to dream there was more to life than what was inside the borders of the Bar M Ranch. That there was more to life than a senseless feud. I thought you'd come with me." He strode toward her, his feet eating up the ground between them, his rage building until his face burned with it. "I thought you'd realize you had a life to live, and I was fool enough to think you'd choose to live it with me." He flung out his hand to emphasize his next point.

When he did, Jennie flinched, her eyes wide saucers in her pale face.

Whatever Cameron had been about to say, and all the anger he'd felt building inside a moment ago, streamed out like air from a punctured balloon. All because of that one slight movement. The flinch of fear in Jennie's body language, the flash of terror in her eyes.

Cameron's arm dropped and he stepped back. For a long moment he didn't say anything.

Jennie straightened, her jaw tightening until it twitched.

"Who hit you, Jennie?" He spoke in a soft tone, completely opposite his harsh and angry shouting of a moment before.

"It doesn't matter anymore." She turned her back to him and continued walking down the path toward the pond, her hands stuffed into her pockets, her shoulders hunched.

He went after her, determined to find out what put that stark fear in her eyes. "Who hit you?"

She stopped, and flung her answer over her shoulder without facing him. "You mean besides the man in the barn?"

"Yeah. The man in the barn wasn't facing you when he hit you. Someone you know or knew has hit you while facing him. Tell me who did it." He knew the answer, but wanted Jennie to confirm it in her own words.

Her shoulders rose and fell with a deep breath before she faced him, tears shimmering in her eyes, her mouth pressed into a tight line. "My husband. The man I promised to love, honor and cherish until death do us part. See? I told you it didn't matter anymore. He's dead." She rolled her eyes. "Hell, the bastard died before I could get the divorce finalized." She laughed, the sound more fractured than her usual chuckle. "I know how to pick 'em, don't I?"

Careful not to spook her again, Cameron reached out and cupped her cheek, ignoring the familiar tremor making his hands shake. "Yeah, you know how to pick 'em. A cowardly bastard and a runaway, ex-jock, army guy who couldn't shoot straight to save his life."

"Oh, Cameron. I didn't mean all those things." Her hand covered his. "I was mad."

"You meant them and I deserved it." He touched his index finger to her eyebrow. "Did he do this?"

She pressed her face into his hand. "Yes."

"Bastard." He leaned close and kissed the scar.

A tear trickled from the corner of her eye and Jennie sniffed. "I swore I wouldn't cry around you."

"Didn't your dad tell you it wasn't nice to swear?" He didn't know what came over him, but the soft,

Bambi-eyed look from her toasted-wheat-colored eyes sucked him in and he was helpless to keep from… His head lowered until his lips brushed against hers.

When she gasped and pressed closer, he gathered her into his arms, his lips claiming hers in a gentle kiss, as if she were a fragile china doll, not the tough cowgirl of the Flying W Ranch.

Her fingers feathered across his neck. She deepened the kiss, her lips parting as she traced the edges of his with the tip of her tongue.

Cameron's hands smoothed over her shoulders and down her back until his fingers rested in the hollow above her buttocks. He shuffled closer, wanting to be with her in every sense. The rock-hard evidence of his rising desire pressed into her soft belly. He could become completely lost in Jennie Ward. Why did he ever think he could be impartial and focused when she was around? Duty surfaced as he heard a twig snap. Unwilling to leave it to the chance that it might be squirrels again, he wrenched his lips from hers and scanned the nearby wooded area. Then grasping her shoulders, he set her away. "We can't."

"No. We shouldn't." She shook free of his hands and pushed her shaking fingers through her hair. "There's too much at stake."

She'd hit the nail on the head. If he lost his ability to remain alert and unaffected by the very person he was sworn to protect, he might compromise her life and that of her father.

On the other hand, he didn't want to think about what else he might compromise.

"Come on. We need to get back to the house. It isn't safe out here." He reached for her hand.

Jennie stared at the proffered hand for a moment before slipping hers into it. "I can't hide forever, Cameron. The ranch can't handle itself. With my father out of commission and me locked up, what will get done?"

"You have three able-bodied ranch hands, let them do it. They aren't the ones under the gun."

"No, but the way you're talking, one of them might be the one holding that gun."

"All the more reason for you to stay in the house." Cameron moved along the base of the tree line toward the house, forcing his senses to alert. Too often today, he'd let himself be distracted. He couldn't afford it. Perhaps Evangeline was right and he was too close to Jennie to be proper protection for her. But the thought of relinquishing the task to someone else was not an option he'd consider.

The sound of a horse's hooves pounded along the path toward them.

Cameron grabbed Jennie by the waist and swung her behind a stand of bushes. His heart slammed against his ribs while he held Jennie in the protection of his arms.

As the thundering hooves grew closer, Jennie chuckled. "It's okay, Cameron. It's just Rudy."

She peeled his hands from around her waist, stepped out of the shadows and waved at the oncoming rider.

Cameron crossed in front of her. He still wasn't sure about anyone where Jennie was concerned. She might trust Rudy, but Cameron didn't know him well enough to pass the same judgment.

The young ranch hand yanked back on the reins, slowing the horse so fast it stirred up a cloud of dust.

"Sheriff's here, and he wants to see you, Miss

Jennie," Rudy blurted out before the horse came to a complete stop.

Jennie frowned at Cameron and then turned toward Rudy. "Thanks, Rudy. I'll see you up at the house."

"You want the horse?" he asked.

"No thanks, I'm sure the sheriff can wait until I walk the rest of the way."

Rudy shrugged. "I don't know. He seemed pretty agitated."

Jennie's face paled, but she pushed back her shoulders and gave the young man a hint of a smile. "Don't worry, Rudy. Tell him I'll be there in a minute."

When Rudy had gone, Jennie followed the horse and rider, picking up her pace. "Suppose they've identified the body?"

"Maybe." Cameron didn't like the sound of this and the skin on the back of his neck tingled. He'd had that same feeling when he'd been out on several missions in the jungles of some third world country—as if something bad was just on the other side of the next tree.

"If they've discovered who it is," Jennie continued talking as if thinking out loud, "why would the sheriff be so interested in seeing me again?"

Two squad cars were parked beside the rambling ranch house. Sheriff Hodges stood on the back deck, his hand over his brow to block the sun from glaring into his eyes. When he spotted them climbing the hill toward him, he descended the wooden steps and met them halfway. "Miss Ward, Cameron."

Cameron swallowed the acid rising in his throat. So it was Miss Ward now. Not the easy familiarity of a man who'd known her all her life.

"I just came from the medical examiner's office.

He wanted to see if you recognized this." Sheriff Hodges held out a clear plastic bag. In it was a heavy silver ring like a man's class ring from college or high school.

Cameron didn't care what it was. Standing on the lawn, they were in full view of several hills. Someone could be zeroing in on Jennie as they stood around staring at jewelry. "Could we move this indoors?" Cameron grabbed Jennie's elbow and urged her toward the house.

She didn't budge.

With a glance from one hillside to another, Cameron finally stared at Jennie. "It's not safe—"

His words died when he saw how white her face had turned. "What's wrong, Jennie?"

She closed her eyes and swayed where she stood.

Before she could fall, Cameron hooked his arm around her waist and held her up.

Jennie turned her back to the sheriff and the ring, burying her face in Cameron's chest. "I know that ring," she whispered.

"You do?" Cameron tipped her chin up and stared into her glazed eyes.

"She should." Sheriff Hodges pulled the handcuffs from the pouch on his utility belt.

What the hell was going on? Cameron stared from the cuffs to the sheriff's face, placing his body between the sheriff and Jennie.

"She should know whose ring it is, because it was her husband's. The fire didn't kill him. The bullet to the back of his head did."

Cameron planted his hands on his hips. "What does that have to do with Jennie?"

"Because she was the only other person we know

who was in that barn, we got a warrant from the county judge to search the Flying W. Two detectives from the Colorado Bureau of Investigations Major Crime Unit are already conducting a search of the ranch house and so far they've found a pistol in Miss Ward's bedroom, one that's been fired recently." He popped the cuffs open and held them out to Jennie. "I'm sorry, Miss Ward, but I have to take you in for questioning for the murder of Vance Franklin."

Chapter Nine

Jennie sat in the backseat of the patrol car, a thousand thoughts jumbled into an unthinkable mass in her head with only one surfacing repeatedly. *How?*

"The detective from the Colorado Bureau of Investigations is meeting us at the office to ask you a few questions about the fire and Vance." Sheriff Hodges glanced at her in his rearview mirror before his gaze returned to the road. "I asked them to let me bring you in instead of one of their units."

"Thanks." Jennie almost smiled at her response. She was thanking the lawman for the handcuffs around her wrists and the ride in the back of the sheriff's cruiser into Dry Wash to be locked in jail for who knew how long. She'd been the one almost murdered, not the other way around. The situation was almost laughable if she hadn't wished her husband dead a hundred times during the year she'd been married to him.

Her eye twitched at the thought of all the times he'd hit her with that very ring. The scar that split her right brow was one of the many he'd graced her with.

She'd probably rot in hell for the number of times she'd wished her husband to be run off the mountain roads. When he had, she felt guilty for her wicked thoughts. At the same time, she felt gloriously free.

If he'd died in that accident, how could his body show up in the barn? Eight years ago, she'd identified his lifeless body at the morgue. Although his face had lacerations, she knew it was him. The same light blond hair he kept meticulously neat, the way his nostrils flared and the shape of his eyebrows. How could she mistake him for the wrong man? Following the funeral, he'd been cremated, his ashes scattered in the Colorado wind. "My husband?" The word stuck in her sore throat. Vance hadn't been a husband to her when they were living together. She had a hard time using the word in connection with the man. "It can't be. My husband's dead. I identified his body eight years ago."

"Ms. Ward, I don't know whose body you identified. After we found the inscription on the ring, we matched his teeth to his dental records. Not many people have gold fillings. Vance Franklin's matched right up."

Even when he wasn't working and living off her father's ranch income, Vance insisted on gold fillings. Nothing but the best for Vance Franklin. He wouldn't settle for second-rate. Why he'd chosen her, she didn't know. A country girl wasn't his style. One with a daddy who owned a big ranch…now that made more sense. For a year, she let him hit her, telling herself she deserved it because she'd never loved him. Why she'd agreed to marry him, she still couldn't begin to fathom. She must still have been on the rebound from Cameron even a year after he'd gone.

The last time he'd hit her, had been the final straw. Her father wasn't buying the gash over her eyebrow was from falling off her horse or bumping into a beam in the barn. He'd kicked Vance out of his house and off his land.

Once Vance was out of her life, Jennie could finally see the trap she'd fallen into. That week she filed for divorce. Two weeks later, Vance died in a car wreck. On the one hand, Jennie was spared from an ugly divorce case in court. On the other, Vance left her a mound of debt Jennie hadn't even known about until the creditors started hounding her for money.

While she'd been riding the ranch and helping her father with the day-to-day operations, Vance had been gambling and spending, using credit cards he'd obtained in both his and her name.

Jennie couldn't bring herself to cry at his funeral or mourn his loss. The fact he couldn't hurt her any more had been liberating.

The sheriff pulled up to the old stone building that had been there as long as the town of Dry Wash. Over the years, the building had seen its share of criminals, drunks and murderers inside its cells.

Jennie's chest tightened.

News vans from Denver television stations lined the narrow streets and people with microphones and cameras hovered like so many sharks ready to launch into a feeding frenzy.

This was it. She was being accused of a murder she didn't commit. Jennie Ward, who wouldn't go over the speed limit or jaywalk because it was against the law. Jennie, who'd always done the right thing.

When the sheriff opened the car door for her, the mob descended. Not used to anything more crowded than a corral full of hungry cattle, a surge of panic rose up in Jennie's throat and she almost let it out in a moan.

Then a voice spoke next to her ear. "It's going to be okay."

Cameron stood beside the sheriff's car, his broad shoulders pushing against the crowd of people to make room for her.

With Cameron on one side and the sheriff on the other, Jennie made it through the throng into the sheriff's office. The crowd didn't seem to be any less packed inside than it was outside. The small office was standing room only with half a dozen state troopers and every sheriff's deputy on the small force.

They all started talking at once, the din earsplitting in the close confines of the office.

The sheriff raised his voice above all the others. "Quiet! Let the lady through." He pushed his way through the outer office to the glass door with Sheriff William Hodges stenciled on the glass. Down the hall Jennie could see several faces peering at her from behind the dark steel bars of the jail cells. She recognized one face as that of the town drunk. Soon, she'd be sitting on the hard bunk in a neighboring cell next to these miscreants.

Swallowing the lump in her throat, Jennie squared her shoulders. She could handle this. She was tough, a Ward through and through.

The sheriff stared at Cameron. "We can take it from here, Mr. Morgan." A man flashing a badge from the Colorado Bureau of Investigations had followed them into the sheriff's office and nodded. "We have a few questions we need to ask Ms. Ward."

Cameron stared across at Jennie, his gaze conveying his empathy. "I'm calling Evangeline. She'll fix you up with a lawyer." His eyes narrowed. "You don't have to say anything without your lawyer present. Remember that."

Jennie nodded, the lump in her throat returning, choking off anything she might have said.

When the door closed behind Cameron, Jennie felt more alone than she'd ever felt in her life. She stared at the sheriff, a man she'd known all her life. He wore a mask of professionalism that made him a stranger to her.

Her gaze crossed to the detective from the Colorado Bureau of Investigations. At least here, she didn't know the man, she couldn't feel betrayed by his changed demeanor.

"Ma'am, tell me, in your own words, what happened yesterday evening on the Flying W Ranch."

She folded her hands in her lap and gave him a level stare while her stomach fluttered. "I'm sorry, sir, but I'm not saying anything until I have a lawyer present." She refused to be trapped into admission of a crime she didn't commit.

CAMERON STEPPED OUT of the sheriff's office into the front office area. The noise was too much. He couldn't hear himself think, much less make the call he needed to make to PPS headquarters.

Outside, he was bombarded by the press, trucked, bussed and driven in from Denver. Must be a slow news day that they'd come all the way to Dry Wash for a story.

"How can a man dead and cremated eight years ago appear in the Flying W's burned-out barn?"

He'd like to know the answer to that question, as well. Cameron kept his mouth shut and pushed through the sea of reporters.

"Was Vance Franklin's death eight years ago all an elaborate hoax?"

Looked that way, but he wasn't the one to confirm their supposition. He didn't clear the crowd until he'd gone halfway down Main Street and turned left onto a smaller side street.

There he stopped to flip his cell phone open, punch the speed dial button for Prescott Personal Securities and wait. *Please don't let Angel be a pain.*

"Prescott Personal Securities, Evangeline Prescott speaking."

Relief washed over him. "This is Cameron. Have you been watching the news?"

"No, I just got to the office. What's happening?"

Cameron let out a long breath before he said, "Jennie's been arrested."

Evangeline gasped. "Why?"

"The body found in the barn was Vance Franklin, her husband."

"What do you mean her husband? I thought he died eight years ago?"

"So did everyone else. I don't know what's going on, but I need a backup to keep an eye on Hank Morgan. He's out at the ranch armed to the hilt, but nursing a broken ankle. The man's a sitting duck."

"I'll get someone right out there."

"If you have any connections, see what you can do to get Jennie out of there. She doesn't belong in jail."

"I'll get her out of there. It might take some time."

"I don't want her staying one night in jail."

"I understand. Let me make some calls, and I'll call you right back."

Cameron flipped his phone shut and paced, his mind

back in the sheriff's station, wondering what new ordeal they were subjecting Jennie to.

He glanced at the clock on his phone. Only one minute had passed since he'd hung up. Standing around and waiting wasn't his style. He needed action to channel his adrenaline. His pacing lengthened to the end of the block. After a smart about-face, his cell phone rang and he almost dropped it in his hurry to answer.

"Cameron, my attorney spoke with the county judge. They've set bail at a quarter of a million. Prescott Personal Securities is posting that bail."

"How long before she'll get out of there?"

"A lawyer is on his way out. She doesn't have to say anything without her lawyer present."

"She knows."

"Good. I've also asked Lenny and Cassie to dig into Vance Franklin's records and find out what he's been up to for the past eight years."

"They can do that? The man got away with being dead for a long time."

"Trust them. They're good." Evangeline paused for a moment before asking, "Are you doing all right?"

"I'm fine." Now the legalities were squared away, he wanted to get back to Jennie before anything else happened. "Don't worry about me, worry about Jennie." If his words were terse…tough.

"Right. But I think you're losing your perspective. How will you be able to protect Jennie and Hank Ward if you're too close to them?"

Clamping down hard on his back teeth, Cameron counted to five before answering. "I know what has to be done."

"I'll tell you I've considered swapping you and Jack

more than once in the last twenty-four hours. My gut tells me you're losing your objectivity. That can prove dangerous. No, lethal."

"Pull me from this case, if that's what you think you need to do." His hand gripped the small phone so tightly he was sure it would break. "If you do pull me off protecting Jennie, I'll have no other choice but to quit the agency."

"Is that a threat?"

"No." All anger faded, replaced with a quiet determination. "It's a promise. I won't let anything happen to Jennie Ward."

"Would that be because you still love her?" Evangeline's words were spoken softly, but Cameron heard them as if they'd been shouted.

Did he still love Jennie Ward? Was he willing to admit it?

"I'll let you know when the lawyer arrives." Cameron closed the phone and hurried back to the jailhouse, his thoughts on Jennie.

Grateful for what Evangeline Prescott had done to clear the path for Jennie's release, Cameron wasn't particularly pleased with his boss's concern over his ability to maintain a professional distance and perspective. She constantly reminded them their jobs weren't personal, they were business.

Bull. His responsibility was to keep Jennie Ward alive. His job began with personal. If he had to quit the agency, he'd see Jennie through the attacks and take out anyone who tried to harm her.

As he neared the mass of reporters and news vans, Cameron took a deep breath and plunged in. Since he wasn't coming out of the sheriff's office, they didn't question him, but he overheard reporters speculating in front of live-feed cameras.

"Was Jennie Ward a party to fooling the public into believing her husband died in a car accident eight years ago? Was it for the insurance money? If so, what made her kill him now? Was he blackmailing her?"

Cameron stopped and stared at the woman holding a microphone while her cameraman recorded her and the crowd gathered outside the jailhouse.

The media would crucify Jennie before she got a fair trial. She'd be tried, convicted and hanged before she saw the inside of a courtroom.

Anger simmered just beneath the surface and he fought to maintain his cool. This was what Evangeline had been worried about. With Jennie's life hanging in the balance, he couldn't afford to stir up a ruckus. The foaming-at-the-mouth thrillmongers would be all over him and tie it to Jennie's case.

Cameron pushed through the swarm, stuffing his hands in his pockets to keep from punching someone in the face.

A deputy stood outside the door to the jailhouse blocking Cameron's path.

He stepped up on the porch to take full advantage of his height, placing him in the position of looking down at the lone deputy. "I'm Ms. Ward's bodyguard, I need to see her."

"I don't care if you're the Pope." The deputy crossed his arms over his chest and gave Cameron glare for glare. "No one goes inside without the sheriff's permission."

Clenching his hands in his pockets, Cameron fought for calm. "Then get the sheriff."

The young deputy's eyes narrowed and he backed toward the door. Opening it a couple of inches he yelled inside. "Get the sheriff." Then, as if someone might dive for the open door, he slammed it shut again and straightened.

To keep from tapping his toe impatiently, Cameron counted backward from one hundred in his head. By sixty-five he'd ground a quarter inch off his back teeth. Finally, the door opened and the sheriff stared out at Cameron. "Why are you standing out here? Ms. Ward's been asking about you."

The young deputy didn't glance Cameron's way as he entered the jailhouse.

Sheriff Hodges strode back to the room in the hallway.

"How's she holding up?" Cameron asked, his tone low so as not to garner attention from the other troopers and deputies helping themselves to the coffee.

"She hasn't spoken a word since you left. We've completed fingerprinting and mug shots, but she refuses to answer any questions until her lawyer arrives."

Cameron hid his smile. Jennie could be stubborn when she wanted. He glanced at his watch. The lawyer would be there within the next thirty minutes. "Could I sit with her while she's waiting for her lawyer?"

"I can't let you be alone," the sheriff said.

"That's okay." He'd sit with her in a crowded room, as long as he sat near her. As he passed by the crowd next to the coffeemaker, he grabbed a cupful of water from the cooler.

When the sheriff opened the door to his office, Jennie glanced up. The dark shadows in her eyes lifted and she gave him a tentative smile. "Is that for me?" Her voice was still scratchy from her ordeal the night before. This woman had gone through so much in the past twenty-four hours. Cameron marveled at her strength.

He held out the cup of water. "Thought you could use it."

She took it and sipped its contents for a minute before she spoke again. "What's happening?"

He filled her in on what PPS was doing for her and her father. "Your lawyer should arrive shortly."

Thirty minutes later, the door opened and a man dressed in a charcoal-gray business suit stepped through carrying a briefcase. Before anyone spoke, he handed out his business card. "I'm Clay Waldorf, Ms. Ward's attorney." He glanced down at her, his expression serious and professional. "If she'll agree to my representation."

"Are you the one Evangeline Prescott sent?" Cameron asked.

"Yes, sir." He held out his hand. "You must be Cameron Morgan. Mrs. Prescott told me about you."

Cameron shook the man's hand. No limp greeting here. The man was solid. Jennie was in good hands if Evangeline Prescott recommended him.

Jennie stood and extended her hand to the attorney. "In that case, yes, you may represent me."

The attorney glanced at the detective and the sheriff. "I'd like a few minutes alone with my client. Do you have a room we can use?"

The sheriff pushed away from his position leaning against his desk. "Stay here. We'll leave."

When the sheriff and detective exited, Cameron stood where he was. "Do you want me to stay or go?"

Again, Clay stared at Jennie, his brows raised. "It's up to Ms. Ward."

Jennie didn't meet his eyes. "Please, I'd rather be alone with my attorney."

Cameron hoped he didn't flinch at her words, although the blow hit him like a punch to his solar plexus. He nodded poker-faced and left the room.

After an hour of floor pacing and glaring at anyone who dared to come close to him, Cameron practically jumped when Jennie and her lawyer emerged from the sheriff's office.

Clay approached the criminal investigator. "She's ready to answer your questions."

For the next hour, Jennie, her lawyer and the criminal investigator holed up in the sheriff's office. Cameron could have bitten a hole through the steel bars of the jail cells as hard as he ground his teeth. When they finally emerged, Jennie looked all done in, her soft blond hair hanging in limp strands around her pale face and dark semicircles smudging the skin beneath her eyes.

The sheriff met them at the door. "The county judge set bail and the bail's been posted. You can go home, Ms. Ward."

Jennie stared across at Cameron, her gaze that of a trapped animal desperate to escape. Despite his angry disappointment at being kept out of the initial interview with her lawyer, Cameron couldn't maintain his anger when she looked so beaten.

He cupped a hand around her elbow and ushered her through the office and out into the thinning crowd of reporters. When people closed in on her, he shielded her body with his and hurried her toward his truck.

She didn't speak until they were clear of town and headed toward home. "I'm sorry."

"For what?"

"You're disappointed I didn't let you stay while the lawyer and I talked."

"I'm not disappointed," he lied.

"Still, I need to explain. You and I have had a...relationship in the past. I want to keep that relationship separate from these charges. You shouldn't be dragged through the muck just because you knew me ten years ago."

"Jennie, I've told you before, I can take care of myself."

"Until we're through all this, I think it's best we stick to the original plan. You're the bodyguard. I'm the person you're supposed to protect. Nothing else. It's better for everyone that way."

Her words echoed Evangeline's and they didn't sit any better with Cameron, especially coming from Jennie. But it was her choice, what could he say? "So be it."

Chapter Ten

As soon as Cameron parked the truck next to the ranch house, Jennie pleaded exhaustion. Within a few minutes, she'd showered and hit the sack.

Just as well. Cameron needed the space.

With things the way they were between them, he didn't see any need to sit around and stare at each other or make idle chatter. He had a job to do, he might as well get down to business.

"Think I'll hit the hay, as well." Hank maneuvered the crutches close to his chair and eased up onto them. Once he reached the upright position, he snorted. "I'll be glad when I can burn these darned things."

"You'll do no such thing. No use wasting a good pair of crutches." Ms. Blainey bustled into the room. "I've turned back the covers and the shower's going for you."

"I can do things for myself, woman," Hank blustered, yet his frown wasn't nearly so ferocious.

"I know you can." She adjusted the collar on his shirt. "I just like doing for you. So hush."

Cameron held back a smile. Ms. Blainey knew how to handle the cranky rancher. "Mind if I use your office? I need to log on to the Internet."

Hank frowned. "I suppose. Although, I don't understand what you can get off the Internet you can't get with a phone call, especially since we're on dial-up out here."

"I'll be making some calls, as well. I figure it'll be quieter from the office." The office was located on the opposite side of the house as the bedrooms, convenient for what Cameron planned.

As soon as Hank and Ms. Blainey ambled off to bed, Cameron ducked in Jennie's door to check on her. She was sound asleep, breathing softly in the darkness.

Rather than dwell on how beautiful she was when she slept, Cameron grabbed his laptop and entered Hank's office.

Dialing in to the Internet was a slow and tedious process in this remote location, but Cameron did it and sent an e-mail out to Lenny asking if he'd found anything yet.

While he waited for a response, Cameron dug through the piles of papers on the desktop, searching for anything that might clue him in to what was going on with the Flying W.

Littered across the massive oak desk were the daily receipts of running a ranch. The ledger lay open with entries scratched onto the pages, the last one over a month ago. Not an efficient way to run a business.

But then Hank wasn't a businessman. He knew his way around cattle and horses, but apparently not a business.

Further digging proved what Cameron already suspected. The ranch was losing money hand over fist, with fencing supplies, tractor repairs and veterinary bills topping the expenses. How they hadn't gone bankrupt was beyond him.

Next, he opened a file cabinet and leafed through the different folders. Someone had started a good system, but the folders were aging as though they'd been there a long time. When he reached the one marked Insurance, he noted the papers inside were newer than the others. Lifting the pages out of the file, he read the date on the ranch policy. The date purchased was at the beginning of this year. He rifled through the remainder of the file, but there were no other insurance policies for prior years.

Had Hank taken out this policy earlier this year then had his barn burned to collect the insurance?

Cameron shook his head. No way. The man had faults, but paying someone to burn his barn couldn't be one of them. Hank loved this ranch as much as Tom Morgan loved his. Pride ran deep in what their fathers' fathers had built from nothing. And he wouldn't have done it with the off chance his daughter would be caught inside.

Working his way through the four-drawer file cabinet, Cameron searched for clues, not really knowing what he was looking for. Were the Wards on the verge of bankruptcy? Was someone pushing them that direction in order to force them to sell? And why had Vance Franklin shown up in that barn with a bullet in his head?

The bottom drawer yielded another surprise that had Cameron taking a seat.

The file dated back over nine years and contained a sheaf of overdue credit card bills and letters from collection agencies threatening to hit Jennie and Vance Franklin with a lawsuit if they didn't pay. Buried between the notices was a clipping of a newspaper article showing a picture of a wrecked sports car, upside down in a ditch. The caption read Local Man Dies in Fatal

Accident. Had Vance Franklin staged his death to get away from creditors? If so, whose body was in the car that was wrecked? Was Jennie a party to the cover-up?

Cameron stayed up into the small hours of the morning searching through every last sheet of paper for anything else that might help determine who was involved in the attempted murders of Hank and Jennie Ward. He never found another insurance policy linking Vance's staged death to Jennie, but that didn't mean it didn't exist, though he couldn't bring himself to believe Jennie would stoop to something as low as insurance fraud. No matter how bad her finances were.

AT THE FIRST LIGHT of dawn creeping through her window, Jennie was up and dressed. If she wanted some time alone, she had to get going before the rest of the ranch woke and tried to talk her out of it. Especially Cameron Morgan, asleep in the room next to hers.

She carried her boots out onto the deck and down the steps before she slid them onto her feet. She had an old bridle tucked behind the seat of the ranch truck. It would fit Mojo, the red Appaloosa gelding, one of the horses she'd been riding since Lady's mishap with the razor blade. As for a saddle? Well, she'd ridden bareback most of her young life. She could do it again.

She needed the wind of the hills blowing through her hair to clear the twitchy, on-edge feeling she couldn't shake. After she collected the bridle from the truck, careful to open and close the doors quietly, Jennie hurried down the hill toward the pasture with the workhorses.

Mojo stood in the south pasture, his head craned between the wood rails of the fence, tempted by fresh green grass on the other side.

When Jennie approached, Mojo raised his head and nickered, sniffing the air for the expected treat.

"Sorry, Mojo. No treat today. Maybe later." She stepped between the rails and slipped the bridle over Mojo's head.

The horse tossed his head cantankerously, but soon settled the bit between his teeth, his mouth working the metal until it fell behind his tongue.

Jennie adjusted the straps over his ears and loosened them beneath his chin. She should run a currycomb over his back, but she was afraid to take the time. She might be forestalled and forced back into the ranch house. At which point, she'd have a raging claustrophobic attack and everyone would point the finger at her for the crazy woman she was becoming.

After being surrounded by people for the past two days, she needed time alone doing what she liked best—riding through the foothills of the Rockies.

With a few comforting words to the horse, she brought the animal beside the wood fence and climbed aboard.

Mojo whinnied, unused to being ridden bareback.

Holding her breath, Jennie glanced up at the house. So far, no one stirred. The gray light of predawn melted into the pink, purple and orange flames of sunrise. Doug, Stan and Rudy would be up by now, fixing coffee in the bunkhouse, and Ms. Blainey would already be out of bed, preparing breakfast for everyone.

Which gave Jennie only a minute or two to make good her escape. She couldn't believe her luck at getting out the door without disturbing Cameron. The man must have radar for ears.

Jennie rationalized that if everyone else was asleep

at this ungodly early hour, it stood to reason so too would be the potential killer. Which gave her a chance to get away from everyone and everything for just a few minutes. She needed the downtime to think through all the craziness of the past few days.

She walked Mojo down the hill and out of sight of the house, before she gave him his head and let him race like the wind.

Her hands twisted in his mane, Jennie leaned low over the Appaloosa and inhaled the earthy scent of horse, loving the feel of power beneath her. On Mojo she could run away from all her problems.

The thought brought her up short and she slowed her headlong flight. When she glanced around at the lush green grasses and the tall cottonwoods, she sighed. Had the horse come here on its own, or had her subconscious led her to the one place she'd avoided for ten years? The place she and Cameron first made love. The quiet copse of trees with the brook running through it was halfway between the Flying W and the Bar M ranch houses. A perfect place to meet on a warm summer's day. She and Cameron had met there often when they were teens. A hideaway from their demented family feuding.

The clear mountain stream gurgled through the valley and just beyond that clump of trees was a shady pool with a small waterfall spilling out of the mossy hillside.

She nudged the horse forward, forcing herself to face the one place she couldn't for so many years. As she rounded the trees, a motor revved to life.

Who the hell was out here at this time of day? Before she could locate the sound, a four-wheeler raced toward her and Mojo.

Mojo screamed and reared, his front hooves rising high into the air.

With no stirrups to press against and only a tenuous hold on a tuft of mane, Jennie slid down the vertical slope of Mojo's back and crashed to the ground. The back of her head smacked against a rock and her world went black.

THE RICH AROMA of brewing coffee jerked Cameron's senses to attention as though just the promise of caffeine was enough to bring him back to life. He lifted his face off the hard surface and glanced around Hank Ward's office where he'd finally nodded off somewhere after three in the morning. Sunlight streamed through a crack in the blinds. What time was it?

Cameron leaped to his feet, his first thoughts on Jennie and Hank. He'd slept on the opposite side of the house. Anything could have happened through the night and he wouldn't have heard.

He almost ran into Ms. Blainey in the hallway on his way to check on Jennie.

"Oh, there you are. Tell Jennie breakfast will be ready in five minutes, will you?"

"Why don't you tell her?"

"I assumed she was with you since you both weren't in your rooms."

His lungs tightening, Cameron grasped Ms. Blainey's shoulders and set her out of his way. His heart in his throat, he ran down the hallway to Jennie's room and threw the door open so hard, the handle banged against the wall. The blinds were open, the bed was made and Jennie wasn't anywhere in sight. No sign of forced entry or a scuffle, but that didn't mean anything. Someone could have gotten her in the middle of the night and he wouldn't have known.

Cameron pushed through the unlocked French doors leading out onto the deck in time to see the tail end of a horse carrying a woman with a long blond ponytail disappear below the hill.

Against all his warnings, Jennie Ward was riding away without an escort. Without him.

"Damn!" Anger flashed through him, followed quickly by fear for Jennie's life. Cameron swung around and raced back into Jennie's room and through to his own where he pulled on his boots.

Ms. Blainey stood out in the hallway. "I'll keep your breakfast warm. Bring that girl back."

Without responding to the older woman, Cameron ran outside to where the vehicles were parked, yanked his saddle from the bed of his pickup and collected a bridle from the backseat. He was across the yard, loping toward the nearby pasture where several horses stood next to the fence, watching him. He'd accomplished this in less than five minutes, but with Jennie, every minute counted. She knew this ranch better than he did. She could lose herself over any one of the hills, valleys or ravines scattered across three thousand acres without even trying.

The horses weren't familiar with him and it took several attempts before a large black gelding strutted within range where Cameron could grab his halter. From there it was a matter of moments before he had the horse saddled, bridled and ready to go.

Swinging into the saddle, he reined the horse toward the north and set off on the most jolting ride he'd ever experienced. The horse had the gait of a camel, but he was fast. Despite his initial discomfort, Cameron and the gelding flew across pastures, through the trees and over hilltops.

Jennie had been headed north the last time he'd seen her. She'd been bareback which meant she wouldn't be going very far or she'd be at a gallop or walk. Trotting was too wearing on the...

Cameron kicked his horse's flanks. Either way, she'd been out of sight far too long. As he raced down a hill, he thought of the places he knew she might have gone in that direction. Only one came to mind. A place nestled in a valley with a little waterfall spilling out of the rocks into a clear blue-green pool of water, so clear you could see to the bottom over ten feet below.

Would she remember that particular location as a happy place? A place they'd made love for their very first time?

Cameron always considered the pool a magical place, all because of Jennie.

With no sign of Jennie or her horse, he headed for the pool and hoped that's where Jennie was. If not, he had another 2900 acres to search to find her.

As he topped the rise leading into the valley, a sound incongruous with the surrounding tranquility echoed off the hillsides. The noise was like that of a motorcycle, but with the echo resonating off rocky cliffs, Cameron couldn't pinpoint the vehicle's location.

Adrenaline ripped through his system and he dug his heels into the gelding's flanks. The horse leaped forward, sliding down the hillside into the valley where the pool was hidden behind a stand of trees. Part of Cameron wished Jennie wasn't there, afraid whoever had sped away on the motorized vehicle had done her harm.

If she wasn't there, he had no other idea where to look.

His answer came to him in the form of a riderless horse racing out of the trees toward him, headed back to the pasture by the house.

Cameron never slowed his pace until he neared the tree line. Then he pulled hard on the reins and slowed his horse to a walk, easing his way along the narrow trail to the pool. On the other side of a clump of brush, he found Jennie.

She lay as still as death, her eyes closed and her face pale.

Cameron leaped off the horse and dropped to the ground beside her. "Jennie," he called out to her, touching a hand to her shoulder, afraid to move her in case she'd been injured in her fall.

No movement, nothing. He pressed two fingers to her throat and waited, counting the seconds until he felt her pulse, a strong, steady beat.

Jennie tilted her head to the side and winced. "What happened?"

He laughed, his relief overshadowing his initial anger at her disappearance. "I don't know. You tell me."

Chapter Eleven

Jennie sat up. Her head throbbed as if a freight train had rolled over it several times.

When she swayed, Cameron wrapped his arm around her shoulder and steadied her. "Are you okay? Feel like anything's broken?"

"Just my head." She moaned and pressed her hands to her temples. "You don't have any painkillers handy, do you?"

"Sorry, fresh out." He swept a strand of hair out of her face. He was tender when he should have been flat-out angry at her for taking off.

"I'm sorry," Jennie said. "I shouldn't have run off without you."

"No, you shouldn't have."

"I just needed some air and time to think."

"I know."

"So you're not mad at me?"

"Yes, I'm mad at you." He leaned forward and gently probed the back of her head until he found the sore spot where she'd hit the rock. "You have matching goose eggs on the back of your head."

"Tell me something new." She gave him a narrow-eyed look. "Hey, how come you're not yelling at me?"

"I should be."

"But you're not."

"Probably because I'm out of breath from my crazy ride to find you."

"How many places did you have to look?"

He straightened to his full six foot three inches, blocking the light trickling through the tree branches. His face was effectively shadowed. "One."

"Oh." So he'd thought of the same place she had. Jennie didn't question further. She didn't want to know why he'd think she would head to this magical place. Could it be that it held the same fond memories for him? The throbbing in the back of her head didn't feel quite so painful, and she was able to climb to her feet without his help.

He brushed grass from her shoulder. "You ready to tell me what happened?"

"I needed some air so I came out here. I thought it was early enough that no one, not even a demented killer would be up and about." She shrugged. "I was wrong."

His fingers clamped on her upper arms and he stared down at her. "Did you get a look at him?"

Jennie closed her eyes against the intensity of his green gaze and pictured the last thing she saw before she'd slid from the back of her horse. "All I saw was a man on a four-wheeler wearing a dark helmet."

"What did the four-wheeler look like?"

"Dark, maybe black, with a winch on the front of it." She gave Cameron a lopsided smile. "I only got a glimpse. The trail is barely wide enough for one animal or one vehicle. He was coming out when I was going in. My horse spooked, so the vehicle got the right of way."

"Did he shoot at you?"

Jennie ran her hands over her arms automatically checking for wounds. "Not that I know if. As soon as I hit the ground, the lights went out."

"We need to get you to the hospital."

"No." She pulled out of his arms and turned toward the pool. "He didn't know I was coming. I didn't tell anyone and I didn't hear a motor following me along the way, only when I got here. I want to know what he was doing down by the pool. Is he our murderer, or was he just out to swim in the pool?"

Cameron's lips pressed together. "You should be in a hospital. You probably have a concussion."

"So what's new? I'm not going back to Denver to spend another night in a hospital. I want to know what the hell's going on."

With a sigh, Cameron grabbed his horse's reins. "Have it your way. Lead on."

Jennie rounded the bend in the trail, unprepared for the beauty she'd avoided for so long. If anything, the clear water of the pool was cleaner, and the vegetation greener and more lush than when she and Cameron swam naked in its depths over a decade ago. Her breath caught in her throat at the image of their young bodies gliding through the clear water. "I haven't been here since…"

"The last time we were together?" Cameron's softly spoken words finished the sentence she hadn't realized she'd spoken aloud.

Water tumbled from the waterfall on the far end of the pool where cliffs rose up forming one wall of the valley. Dark, craggy rocks coated in moss shone in a light sheen of spray and spindly trees clung to the staggered rock face of the cliff.

Jennie walked out to the water's edge and stared across the smooth surface of the deep green water. "What was he doing here?"

Cameron tied the horse to a tree and then squatted close to the ground. "I don't know but it looks like he dragged something along the dirt here." He pointed to where gouges in the dirt led to the pool close to where Jennie stood.

Jennie's gaze followed the tracks. "Is that blood?" She pointed at the dark brown spots along the way. Her stomach fluttered and she turned her attention back to the pool, staring down into the water in front of her. Still murky, the sediment was just beginning to settle and the shape of an animal could be seen.

Cameron peered over the rock ledge. "Looks like a goat."

"But why throw a dead animal into the pool?"

His glance veered to the lower end of the pool where it trailed out into a stream and Cameron straightened. "Where does the stream lead?"

"It flows south into a livestock watering hole about two hundred yards downstream."

"Where does the majority of your herd drink?"

"Right now?" Jennie's eyes widened. "At that watering hole. It's the only one in this area."

"Looks to me like he was dumping the dead goat into the water to poison the watering hole. A few days from now, your cattle would be getting sick."

"Damn." Jennie shook her head. "He was trying to poison our livestock."

"Good thing you showed up to find the goat before the animal decomposed. You up to giving me a hand?" Cameron strode to his saddle and untied the rope hanging from the side.

"Sure."

He looped the rope around the saddle horn and turned the horse away from the pool. "Stand here with the horse. When I say go, walk the horse away from the water."

"Okay."

Then Cameron unbuttoned the blue chambray shirt he wore, stripped it from his shoulders and tossed it over the saddle.

Blood rushed through her system as Jennie fought not to stare at the broad expanse of muscles.

The boots came next. When Cameron stood in front of her with his hands on the button to his jeans, he smiled. "Do you mind?"

She wanted to say something flippant like, *It isn't as if I haven't seen you naked before.* But her face flamed, her tongue tied and she turned away before he could see how hot and confused he made her.

The sound of denim dropping to the ground took her breath away.

Then a splash indicated he'd jumped into the water and the rope tied to the saddle pulled tight.

Jennie risked a glance into the pool.

Cameron stood in water that came up to his waist, the silt stirred up by his movement disguising anything else of interest below the surface. Rivulets streamed over his shoulders, making his skin glisten in the dappled lighting.

If there hadn't been a dead goat at the bottom of the pool, Jennie might have been tempted to join Cameron.

Not until the dead animal began decomposing would it poison the water, but still…the idea of swimming with a dead goat was just…creepy. Besides, they had a job to do, she didn't need the distraction of his naked chest to derail her.

After taking a deep breath, Cameron dived beneath the surface.

For the full minute and a half he was submerged, Jennie held her breath.

When he surfaced, he scrubbed a hand over his face and nodded. "I've got the legs tied, you can pull it out."

Glad for relief from staring at his chest, Jennie clucked her tongue and tugged the horse's reins until he moved forward, lifting the dead goat out of the pool.

Once it was on dry land and several yards from the clear green waters, Jennie said, "Whoa."

She turned toward Cameron to ask if she'd moved it far enough.

He had just climbed from the water and was reaching for his discarded clothing.

Naked as the day they'd made love in this spot, his body was even more magnificent than ten years ago. His broad shoulders had widened and the muscles stretched taut over his torso. Water glistened in the smattering of dark hair sprinkled across his chest that dipped south to a narrow waist. Not an ounce of fat graced the hard, muscular ripples across his abdomen.

As her wandering gaze drifted downward, her blood heated and she couldn't look away. How long had it been since she'd made love to a man? To this man? Too long. An ache spread throughout her body, reminding her she was still alive, and she still had needs her husband had never been able to satisfy.

Her husband. The man shot in the head and burned in the barn where she'd almost perished.

Jennie turned away and waited for Cameron to complete dressing.

With his light blue shirt clinging to his body, Cameron joined her beside the horse. "I'll take it from here."

The smell of fresh water on male skin overwhelmed her for a moment and clouded her thinking. "What are you going to do with it?" What was she going to do with her lusting thoughts about a man she couldn't—shouldn't—have?

"I'm going to drag it out into a field, far enough away from the pool it won't cause any more harm. There aren't any identifying marks on the goat—no ear tags or brands. It could be from any number of ranches around."

"Including ours. We have a small herd of Spanish goats."

Cameron knelt beside the goat. "Looks like someone slit its throat."

Jennie flinched. It was one thing to raise animals for food, another to brutally kill an animal with the intent of poisoning an entire herd. "Not only are they trying to kill me and my father, they're trying to kill our herd." She grounded her hands on her hips and stared out at the peaceful valley, rage humming inside. "Bastard."

"Come on. We need to get back to the ranch. I don't like the idea of you being a target for our guy on the four-wheeler."

Cameron led the horse out into the valley and untied the goat. "I'll have one of the hands come back with a shovel and bury it. Right now, I want to get you home."

At first, Cameron's concern grated on her. She was used to operating independently. But with the attempts on her life and now the attempt on her herd, she was beginning to appreciate her bodyguard's presence. "What I don't get is, if the guy who dumped the goat into our water supply is the same one who's trying to kill me and Dad, why didn't he finish me off instead of running?"

Cameron's lips tightened. "I don't know. I doubt he saw me coming or heard me over the sound of his engine. It doesn't make much sense." He climbed into the saddle and reached a hand down to her. "I'm just glad he didn't."

As she grasped his large hand, warmth spread up her arm and throughout her body. She slid onto the horse's back behind the saddle and wrapped her arms around Cameron's waist, pressing her face against his still-damp back.

As the horse took off at a trot, Jennie was jolted back to reality. "You had to pick Little Joe from all the other horses?" she grumbled, her teeth clattering together.

Without the benefit of stirrups, she couldn't post to keep her bottom from bouncing against the horse every agonizing step it took.

"He's the only one who'd come up to me. I took what I could get. Not the smoothest gait, but he's fast."

"Great." She settled against him, her head beginning to throb all over. Just as well—she needed a rough reminder to get all romantic thoughts of Cameron out of her mind, including the image of him standing naked in the water. He was only there to be her bodyguard. Nothing more.

WITH HIS ATTENTION on every shadow along the trail, Cameron couldn't help but appreciate the feel of

Jennie's arms around his waist. Almost too much. By the time they reached the ranch, the heat generated between the two of them steamed his clothing dry.

He stopped at the front porch to let Jennie off.

Before he could help her, she slid from the horse's back and climbed the steps. "I'll get one of the hands to take that horse."

"No need. I've got a brush and currycomb in my truck. You go inside. It'll only take me a few minutes."

He needed that few minutes to unwind from the ride home. His jeans were tight and uncomfortable, not that a few minutes would help that much. A cold shower might be next on his list. Especially after diving into a pond with a dead animal.

After a quick brush down, he let the horse loose in the south pasture with the other horses. He'd just laid his saddle in the bed of his pickup when he heard someone calling his name.

"Cameron!" Ms. Blainey stood on the porch, waving the cordless phone. "Telephone. It's someone from Prescott."

"Coming." He tossed the bridle in on top of the saddle and loped back to the house. Ms. Blainey handed him the phone and ducked back inside.

"Cameron?" Lenny's voice sounded urgent.

"Yeah. What's up?"

"Found out something interesting about the dead man in the barn."

"Franklin?"

"Yeah." Lenny paused.

Cameron held his breath, ready to ask, if Lenny didn't get to his announcement quickly.

"He had an identical twin named Lance Franklin."

Jennie stepped out on the deck, her forehead creased in a frown.

Cameron stared at her over the phone, relieved by the news, his mind racing down several possible paths and scenarios. He whispered to her, "Did you know Vance had a twin?"

Her frown deepened and she shook her head. "He told me he was an only child."

"Hey, Lenny. He didn't bother to tell his wife about his brother."

"Here's another interesting fact. Lance's parents had him committed to a mental institution when he was eighteen for suicidal behavior. While in the institution, his parents died. His brother, Vance, had him released two weeks before he supposedly died in a car accident."

"Wow."

"Wow, what?" Jennie leaned closer to listen, pressing her ear to the phone.

"And where is Lance Franklin now?" He bet he knew the answer.

"There's a current address here in Denver. I have one of the agents checking into it as we speak."

"He won't be there."

"That's what I'm thinking."

"I'll bet Vance traded places with his brother and staged the accident."

Lenny laughed. "Great minds think alike."

"Find out more—"

"About the fake Lance Franklin's activities?" Lenny jumped in and finished the sentence. "I'm already on it. More later, Cam."

"Thanks for the info, Lenny."

"A twin?" Jennie's brows rose. "Vance had a twin?"

That edgy feeling that they were being watched crawled across Cameron's skin. He glanced at the nearby hills. "Come on. Let's go inside."

Once in the living room with Hank and Jennie, Cameron paced.

"Why the hell you can't keep an eye on my daughter, I don't know. You're obviously not good at being a bodyguard if you can't keep up with the body you're supposed to guard."

"Quit your bellyaching, Hank Ward." Ms. Blainey entered with a tray of lemonade and glasses and stopped in front of Cameron. "Have a drink before you wear out the flooring."

Cameron shook his head and continued his pacing, ignoring Hank's cantankerous remarks.

Jennie accepted a glass of lemonade and the two painkillers Ms. Blainey held out. "Why would Vance keep a thing like having a twin brother from me?"

"That lousy excuse for a husband had a twin? I knew he was a liar. A cheat, a liar and a wife beater. That boy was full of hidden talents." Hank slammed his palm to the arm of his chair. "If that son of a bitch was still alive, I'd shoot him myself."

Cameron stopped pacing and stared across at Jennie. "I suspect he didn't want to tell his prospective bride he had a twin in a mental institution."

"Think he was afraid I might have changed my mind?" Jennie nodded. "It explains a lot. I'm surprised Vance's parents didn't put Vance in the institution—he was the mental case."

Hank snorted. "Any man who likes to hit women belongs in an institution."

"Agreed," Cameron said, his gaze fixing on Jennie.

Jennie ignored his look and laid a hand on her father's shoulder. "He's gone, Dad. He's not going to hurt anyone anymore."

"He was bad from the start. I don't understand what you saw in him." Hank jerked his head in Cameron's direction. "For that matter, I don't get what you see in Morgan, here. He's given you nothin' but grief."

"Dad." Jennie's voice was tight, her face drawn and angry. "Cameron isn't Vance. He'd never hurt another person."

"Yeah, that's why he was in the Special Forces." Hank crossed his arms over his barrel chest. "I suppose you didn't hurt anyone while in the army, did you? I also suppose you didn't carry a rifle and shoot people."

Cameron refused to be drawn into an argument he knew he stood no chance of winning. Hank was out to pick a fight.

Ms. Blainey planted her fists on her hips and glared at Hank. "This line of talk isn't getting you any closer to figuring out who's after you and Jennie."

"I don't want Jennie making the same mistake with Morgan as she did with Vance."

"I'm not making any mistakes and Cameron isn't Vance, so stop comparing them. They're nothing alike."

"Then why did he leave you and make you cry. Tell me that, will you?" Hank turned to Cameron. "Why did you leave my little girl and make her cry? I should have gone after you and shot you for making her cry."

Cameron bit back his retort and stared at Jennie. Had she cried when he'd left? What a bastard he'd been. She must have hated him for forcing her to choose.

"You made my baby girl cry. For that I won't forgive you."

Jennie shook her head, bright spots of red coloring her cheeks. "It's not for you to forgive, damn it! It was my life and my choice to stay behind with you."

Cameron felt like he was eavesdropping on a private conversation and he turned toward the door. "I'll leave you two to your argument."

"Like you left my daughter?" Hank demanded. "What kind of choice was that?"

"Did you not hear me?" Jennie stood between Hank and Cameron. "I chose not to go with him. I chose to stay with you."

Hank stared at her, his white brows wrinkled on his forehead. "What do you mean?"

"He asked me to go with him. I chose to stay."

Her father's face appeared to age, the color turning a sickly gray. "Because of me?"

"Yes." Jennie's shoulders sagged and she looked at him, tears in her eyes. "I couldn't leave you here alone."

"So now I'm a charity case?" Hank's voice rose with each word. "Of all the pigheaded—" His tirade ended in a grunt of pain and he clutched at his chest.

"Dad?" Jennie hurried toward her father. "What's wrong?"

"Chest hurts." The words came out in a gasp, his face twisting into a grimace.

With frantic, jerky movements Jennie sifted through the newspapers and remote controls on the end table next to his chair. "Where's your Nitrolingual spray?"

Hank waved with one hand. "Night table."

Nitrolingual spray? Nitro? It took half a second for the words to sink in and Cameron lifted the cordless phone he'd used a moment ago. His hands shook as he punched the keypad with the numbers 9-1-1.

Jennie raced down the hallway and was back in a matter of seconds, carrying a spray cylinder. She yanked off the white cap and held the container in front of her father's face. "Open your mouth, Dad."

Hank shook his head. "I don't need it. I'm fine."

"Like hell you are. Open your damn mouth, now!" Jennie stood with her chin jutting out and her eyes blazing.

Cameron was amazed when Hank opened wide like a child receiving cough medicine.

Jennie placed the can close to his lips and sprayed a red liquid into his mouth.

As he watched the drama in the living room, the county dispatcher answered his call on the first ring. Cameron spoke softly, explaining the situation and asked for an ambulance.

Only after Hank took his nitro spray did Jennie relax enough to look at Ms. Blainey. "Call the ambulance. We're taking him to the hospital."

"I'm not going to the hospital. You're getting all excited about nothing but a little gas." Hank lay back against the lounge chair, his face a pasty grey.

"The hell you're not." Jennie marched toward Cameron. "Give me that phone."

"I tell you, there's no use calling the ambulance."

"Too late, Mr. Ward. There's one on the way as we speak." Cameron clicked the off button and handed the phone to Jennie.

She gave him a strained smile. "Thanks."

As she took the phone from him, he grasped her hand. "Answer one question for me."

"No." She pulled against his grip but Cameron wasn't letting go.

"When did your father start having heart problems?"

Chapter Twelve

Cameron hadn't spoken two words since Jennie told him her father had had heart problems for over ten years. She'd ridden in the ambulance to the hospital, not because she was afraid her father would pass on, but to avoid the stony silence of riding with Cameron.

All the way there, she'd peered through the windows in the back door at the stern-faced man driving the black pickup behind them all the way to the hospital. Cameron's black pickup with the smashed front grill.

So she hadn't told him her choice was because her father had a bad heart. What difference would it have made? Cameron needed to leave. He'd always needed to get away from the ranch and the feud that ate at his insides. Without her around, he could have patched up his relationship with his father and brother.

Yet, during the ten years he'd been gone, Molly had kept Jennie informed. The men still weren't talking. They never forgave Cameron for seeing Jennie, and they'd hated him even more for leaving his heritage behind.

What a waste. Sitting next to her father, she knew how much family meant. She'd lost her mother, she'd be damned if she'd lose her father any time soon.

Once they had her father stabilized in the Cardiac Intensive Care Unit, it was past visiting hours and the nurses shooed her out.

Cameron waited in the hallway by the elevator.

She couldn't avoid the inquisition any longer. When Jennie finally emerged from her father's room, Cameron stood talking to a pretty brunette wearing a crisp white nurse's uniform, her hair pulled back in a neat bun at her nape.

"Jennie, this is Sara Montgomery from Prescott Personal Securities. Mrs. Prescott sent her over to protect your father while he's in the hospital."

"You're a bodyguard?"

The woman nodded, a smile lifting her lips. "That's right. The outfit is just a disguise. I don't know a bedpan from a scalpel."

Relief washed over Jennie. "Good. I wasn't sure how that would work. As tight a ship as they run here in the CICU, I don't think the nurses are up to fending off a murderer after one of their heart patients. Nice to meet you, Sara." Jennie held out her hand and gave the woman a tired smile. Next to her, Jennie felt every bit the filthy ranch hand she was. "I'd like to say I don't always look this bad, but it would be a lie."

The woman laughed, her green eyes sparkling. "You look great, and for the record, I love the smell of horses."

So not only did she look like a wreck, she smelled like the inside of a barn. Jennie sank slowly into a tired wallow of self-pity, the stress of her father's heart attack weighing heavily on her.

"Is he going to be all right?" Cameron asked.

"They'll run an arteriogram tomorrow to see where

the blockage or damage has occurred." She was tired and bone weary of running from mysterious bad guys. "Can we go home? They won't let me stay anyway."

"I'd like to run by the office before we go to the ranch."

"Fine. I'll wait out in the truck."

"Wrong. You don't get it." He cupped her elbow and escorted her into the elevator, pressing the first floor button. "Someone wants you dead. You'll come inside with me. But first, I want a doctor to look at you."

After another hour and a half in the emergency room, armed with a doctor's cautionary okay to leave, they drove across town to the Prescott Personal Securities building in the heart of downtown Denver. Cameron parked in the covered parking garage in the lower levels of the building.

"Prescott Personal Securities has offices here?" Jennie stepped into the spacious lobby. With floors tiled in rich granite and a massive front desk manned by two security guards, the entrance was ostentatious and somewhat intimidating.

"Yes, they do. On the top floor."

As they approached the guards, Jennie was even more aware of her bedraggled appearance.

Cameron didn't appear at all discomfited by his casual cowboy clothing and dusty boots.

If he wasn't worried about the filth and grime, then why should she worry? As she walked through, Jennie pushed her tired shoulders back and held her head high.

After Cameron showed his badge and Jennie gave her name and driver's license number, the guards smiled a greeting and waved them through.

Even the insides of the elevator were fancy with brass handrails. Glass walls overlooked downtown Denver, the view improving steadily as they rose above the Denver skyline. A million lights glowed in the gathering dusk like a flutter of magical fireflies. Jennie felt like the country bumpkin on her way to the queen's palace dressed in her dirty jeans.

When the elevator reached the top floor, they stepped out to face a heavy glass door. Cameron waved at the woman on the other side, who promptly buzzed them through. Inside, the office was decorated in a more relaxing style of soft earth tones and terra-cotta decor giving the waiting area a soothing quality. Southwest motifs of Native American paintings and desert landscapes soothed the eye and put Jennie more at ease. Since it was already after ten o'clock, she didn't expect to see a receptionist; the young woman sat behind the desk, glancing up for a moment to smile a greeting, before her gaze returned to the monitor.

"Do you always have a receptionist on duty?"

"Always. And each is trained in self-defense, even our misfit, Angel." Cameron cupped her elbow and led her down the cubicle-filled aisles, with only the occupied offices lit. A bright light shone from the inside corner office. Apparently, their destination.

"That'll be Lenny, one of our computer gurus." Cameron led the way through the maze of cubicles to a brightly lit room in the corner, lined with computers and display screens.

A tall gangly man with red hair and a profusion of large red freckles buzzed them through the locked door of the computer room. He straightened from his chair in front of a computer screen and held out his hand. "Cameron."

Cameron took the man's hand and smiled warmly. "Hey, Lenny. Got any news?"

"As a matter of fact, I've just been sifting through all of Lance Franklin's, aka Vance, financial records." Lenny shoved a hand through his overlong curly red hair making it stand on end like a cheap clown's wig. "The man was in serious debt. From the number of ATM withdrawals at Vegas and Reno casinos, he had a gambling problem. Talk about your super loser."

Jennie snorted. "Sounds like something Vance would do."

Lenny looked at her as if seeing her for the first time. "You knew him?"

"Yes, unfortunately I was married to the man, however brief the union." She held out her hand. "I'm Jennie Ward. Formerly known as Jennie Franklin."

Lenny's face suffused with a bright red turning all his freckles an even deeper shade of orange. "I'm sorry."

She smiled at the man. "You and me both. It was a lapse in judgment on my part."

"That's something about him faking his death by killing off his brother."

"I didn't even know he had a twin. When I identified the body at the morgue, it looked just like Vance, the blood type matched. He was dead." Vance had always been a reckless driver and Jennie had been so glad it was all over, she hadn't thought to question whether or not the man wasn't who she thought he was. "He skipped town and left me with all of his gambling debts to pay off." Another reason the ranch wasn't in as good a financial condition as it could have been. For the past ten years, she'd been paying down the debts her husband had incurred during their one-year marriage.

Cameron's hand on her arm only reminded her of her

poor choices. Whereas Cameron was an honorable man, Vance had been a liar, a cheat and an abuser, just like her father said. Jennie shook her arm free and stepped away from him.

"Come see this." Lenny took his seat at the computer and brought up a screen. "This is a list of recent bank transactions made by our friend Lance, aka Vance, Franklin. Look at some of these larger sums of money coming in and going out."

"Do you know where from and where to?" Cameron asked.

"I'm still digging. I'll give you the skinny when I know more. But whatever it was he was involved in got him killed. Although I can't see that he was that big of a loss to society."

Good riddance. Jennie didn't say it, but she sure felt it. The man had given her nothing but grief and done nothing but aggravated her father's heart condition when he'd lived with them.

"Unfortunately, we didn't get to interrogate him." Cameron's lips were tight when he spoke the words. "It might have made the search go a little faster."

"Then again, he might have sent us on wild-goose chases. The data will paint a clearer picture." Lenny cracked his knuckles and pressed his fingers to the keyboard. "If you'll excuse me, I have to find some money."

"Before you go back to your search, could you rig Jennie with a tracking device?"

Lenny chuckled and grinned from ear to ear. "Having trouble keeping up with her?" He winked at Jennie. "Does a body good to see the great Cameron Morgan resort to a tracker to keep up with a woman."

Lenny's wink and comments didn't take the sting out of Cameron's request and Jennie wasn't one to keep her mouth shut. "I don't need a tracking device."

Crossing his arms over his chest, Cameron gave her a narrow-eyed glare. "After what happened this morning, I can't trust you to stay where you're supposed to stay."

Jennie's lips tightened into a thin line. "I'm not a child you can keep on a tether."

"More's the pity." Cameron inhaled and let it out. "No, really, think about it. You live on a three-thousand-acre ranch. If you take off again, I can't spend all day looking for you. This morning worked out okay. We might not be so lucky next time." When Jennie opened her mouth to protest more, Cameron cut her off with a raised hand. "Please. I'd feel a whole lot better knowing I could find you quickly. And I know your father would feel a lot better knowing that I could track you down if I had to."

The whole idea of having a tracking device rankled with her, but Cameron had a point. Her father would rest easier if he knew they could find her. "You had to play the father trump card, didn't you?"

The corners of his mouth twitched. "I'm catching on. It's only taken me ten years. I must be a slow learner."

"So you're good with it?" Lenny waited for Jennie's nod. When she gave it, he hurried to a black cabinet against the wall and unlocked the door. After rifling through the electronic gadgets and gizmos, he unearthed a device about the size of a small walkie-talkie and another device the size of a dime.

He handed her the tiny disk. "This one is for you. It's only as good as you are at carrying it. It's hardened to take a beating and so it can be submerged in water, but if it's not on your person, it won't do Cameron any good. Understand?"

She nodded and slid it into her jeans pocket.

Lenny handed Cameron the larger device and showed him how to switch it on and read the GPS map to locate her.

"Got it." Cameron slid the tracker into his shirt pocket. "Ready to head home?"

"More than." Her head had started throbbing and she looked forward to a large painkiller and her own bed.

On the ride down the elevator Jennie thumbed the disk in her pocket, a part of her glad she had it and that Cameron was only a GPS unit away from her. With her father in the hospital and her at the ranch, Jennie was beginning to feel more and more exposed to whatever nutcase was out there trying to eradicate what was left of the Ward family. All for what? A piece of real estate? A drought-ridden, money pit of a ranch that barely supported the owners and what remained of the workers. Tomorrow's procedure at the hospital also weighed on her mind. An arteriogram could cause additional stress to her father's heart. Some people died on the table with the so-called simple procedure.

"Worried about your dad?" Cameron ran a hand down her arm, stopping to collect her hand at the bottom. He threaded her fingers through his, just as he had when they were kids.

Jennie's fingers closed with his and she let herself be that kid again, when all they had to worry about was getting caught holding hands by their families. "Yeah, I'm worried about him."

"Why didn't you tell me he had a heart condition back then?"

She shrugged. "What would have changed? You needed to go. I needed to stay."

The rest of the elevator ride concluded in silence. Jennie thought about the choices she'd made and what life would have been like had she gone with Cameron. Would her father still be alive without her and Ms. Blainey to nag him to take his medicine and keep an eye on him when he was having a tough time?

Probably not.

As much as she'd loved Cameron, she couldn't leave her father alone.

THE REVELATION about Hank Ward's heart condition had set Cameron back on his heels. All these years, he'd thought Jennie was afraid to commit to him, when all along, she'd given up her dreams to be there for her father.

Cameron pulled out of the parking garage and drove through the streets of downtown Denver, deep in thought.

Jennie sat silently next to him, staring out the passenger window, her reflection one of a tired, worried woman.

Not until he'd made several turns did he notice the older model dark green or black car keeping pace with them. When he turned onto the road leading to the interstate, he increased his speed. The car behind him leaped forward and was beside him before he could react.

The dull gray barrel of a pistol pointed at him from the window of the rusted-out vehicle.

Instinct kicked in and Cameron slammed his foot onto the brake pedal.

A loud crack sounded and the front windshield shattered where a bullet hit the glass, passed through and narrowly missed Jennie's forehead as she pitched forward in her seat.

"What the hell?" Her hands jerked up to shield her face from flying glass.

Now in front of them, the car skidded sideways, the pistol coming up for round two.

Cameron spun the steering wheel, positioning the driver's side of the vehicle between the pistol and Jennie. At the same time, he gunned the accelerator and leaped over the corner of a sidewalk, mowed down a stop sign and bounded onto a one-way side street. Another shot clanged against the metal bed of the pickup as they rounded the corner and moved out of range of the gunman.

Cameron sped along the deserted city streets, determined to get Jennie out of harm's way. Headlights in his rearview mirror trashed that theory. "Hold on!" At the next corner, he jerked the steering wheel to the left. He needed to get back to the interstate if he wanted to get her home. But the interstate was too wide-open and left them exposed to gunfire from anybody who wanted to take a shot at them.

Cameron would be better off losing them in the twists and turns of downtown Denver. Two streets over, he caught a glimpse of the car, riding parallel to their route. Damn!

Once again, he slammed on the brakes and skidded sideways to a halt. Then he completed the about-face and took off in the opposite direction, headed back the way they'd come. This time, Cameron made a maze of left and right hand turns, carrying him farther away from their persistent shadow. With every twist and turn, the old car kept finding them.

Jennie stared over her shoulder through the back windshield. "Why can't we lose them?"

Cameron slammed a hand to the steering wheel. Why hadn't he thought of it before? Just like the tracking device he had on Jennie, someone had one on them. But where was it?

He sped up and made a few intricate turns, using speed to put enough distance between them and their tail.

"We have to ditch the truck."

"What?"

"The way they're staying so close, tells me they have to be tracking us. I don't have any devices in my pocket."

"I only have the one you gave me."

"Then it has to be the truck." He glanced her way, his lip curling up on one side. "Want to play a little hide-n-seek?"

"I'm game." She slid her hand down to the safety belt latch, ready to push the button. "Say the word and we can run."

Cameron smiled at the excitement lighting Jennie's face, which, a moment ago, was sad. Despite the urgency of the situation and the fact that she'd been thrown from a horse and her father lay in the hospital, she was up for the challenge. If he had time, he'd reach across and hug her. No whining for Jennie. She was one tough cookie and he lov—

The car appeared out of nowhere in front of them, blocking the narrow street. For an old bomb of a vehicle, it got around the streets really well. Not that Cameron had time to ponder the vehicle stretching from sidewalk to sidewalk, blocking the street.

"Duck!"

Several rounds popped off, piercing the windshield to the right of Cameron's head. Instead of spinning around and running the other direction, he slammed his foot to the accelerator and the truck sped forward on its kamikaze path to take out the trouble where it began.

As he braced for the impact and air-bag deployment, Cameron grabbed Jennie's head and pushed it to her knees, hoping he wasn't making a big mistake.

Cameron couldn't see who was inside the other car, but whoever it was had given up shifting into gear and threw himself to the other side of the front seat.

Topping forty miles an hour at impact, the sudden stop slammed Cameron's body forward. The air bag burst from the steering column, bounced against his face, sparing him serious injury from the steering wheel. Immediately, the air bag deflated.

For a full five seconds, Cameron sat in stunned silence, remembering how to breathe. Jennie sat up, her eyes wide, a gash across her face where glass had slashed her skin.

Cameron saw movement in the car and the far door opened. A man tumbled out, wearing a ski mask. He reached back inside the vehicle for something.

Unwilling to wait around to find out what the guy was looking for, Cameron yanked the truck into reverse. Fortunately, it still worked. By the way the steering wheel pulled to the left, he knew he had problems either with the frame, or the front left tire. He could only hope to get a few blocks between him and the gunman before they had to completely abandon his truck.

In the rearview mirror, Cameron saw the man straighten from the crippled vehicle. He laid his forearms over the hood of the car and aimed a rifle at them.

"He's found a gun." Jennie stared over the back of the seat as the man fired.

Cameron reached out and pushed her head to her knees again. "Keep down."

A bullet pierced the rear window and nicked his shoulder. Though the pain was sharp, Cameron knew it was only a flesh wound. He didn't have time to worry about it, he had to get them out of range, and soon.

At the first corner, he turned. With a building between them, he had a few seconds to get the hell away before the man could reach the corner on foot. He gunned the engine.

His breath caught in his throat when the engine sputtered several times before it finally engaged. Leaving a trail of rubber on the pavement, the truck shot forward, the front fender shuddering.

When he finally felt he'd left the man behind, Cameron knew it would only be a matter of time before whoever was following them would find another vehicle and track down the truck. He headed downtown again and parked the truck in the parking garage beneath Prescott Personal Securities. Evangeline always kept a spare sedan at the ready for anyone who needed anonymity while tailing a subject.

Within a matter of minutes, he and Jennie ducked into the PPS office and briefed the staff on duty of what had happened. He left his keys with Lenny and collected a spare set for one of the nondescript sedans. After a long stop at the Denver Police to report the shooting, Cameron grabbed Jennie's elbow and steered her out of the building and into the parking lot. She was dragging by the time they'd settled into the car's interior and left the police station.

Thankfully, no headlights dogged them and they made their way to the interstate without further mishap.

"I can't believe it's already one in the morning." Jennie yawned and pulled the elastic band out of her hair. "Hell, I can't believe less than an hour ago, we were being chased through the streets being shot at."

"Know what you mean. The streets seem calm. Too calm."

Her shoulders shook as if a chill had set in. "No use going back to the ranch. Dad's procedure is at seven in the morning."

"I can't take you to my place. Whoever bugged my truck might know where I live."

"Find a motel or hotel or something. I'm tired." She cast a look his way, her eyes widening. "Cameron, you're still bleeding. Turn this truck around and take us back to the hospital."

"No need. It's only a flesh wound." But he liked that she was worried about him.

"Another reason to stop for the night. There." She pointed to a blue exit sign with a listing of the hotels available. "Pull over and I'll get us a room."

As he slid into the entryway of a Motel 6, his arm shot out to stop Jennie from leaping out. "Just one room. I'm not letting you out of my sight."

Chapter Thirteen

"We got the last room." Jennie slid into the car with two key cards to a room on the well-lit front side of the motel. She hoped they could get a few hours sleep before her father's procedure.

Cameron shifted the car into Drive and pulled around to a parking space close to their room. "I left a message for Sara and told her what happened and to keep a close eye on your father tonight."

"Thanks." Jennie gathered the toiletries she'd collected from the night clerk and led the way to the room.

Cameron glanced over his shoulder every time a car passed the entrance to the hotel.

"Stop that," Jennie said. "You're making me nervous."

"Sorry. After what happened tonight, I'm a bit on edge."

A tense Cameron didn't help settle the knots in Jennie's stomach. Knots put there by a gunman trying his damnedest to put a hole through her. Add to that her fear of being alone with Cameron Morgan. Especially when she was feeling particularly vulnerable and needing the touch of another human. One who could remind her she was still very much alive.

He held the door for her, a smile twitching at the corners of his lips. "Don't worry, I won't bite." As Jennie passed him, she could swear he added "much" to the end of the sentence.

When she looked back at his face, it was poker smooth and he raised his brows as if to say, *What?*

"Did you say something?"

His brows tilted upward. "Only that I don't bite."

"No. After that."

He shook his head, all innocence. "Not that I recall."

Jennie's eyes narrowed. She wasn't reassured by the straight face and guiltless look but she entered the room anyway. "You can have the shower first." Then she glanced at the bed occupying the center of the room and her heart slammed against her chest. "I asked the clerk for a double."

"Looks like a double to me." Cameron's lips stretched into a full grin.

"No, two beds, not a double bed." One bed wouldn't work. There were two of them in the room. One of them Cameron Morgan, ex-football jock and all-around big guy.

"He must have misunderstood."

She turned to retrace her steps to the lobby but was stopped by a long arm stretched across the doorway. "The more you expose yourself, the more likely they'll find us tonight."

"But the bed…" Jennie risked a glance at his face.

"I promise not to touch you, if you don't want me to."

Jennie chewed on her lip. What was she afraid of?

That Cameron would touch her? Or that she'd want him to? "I think I should get the clerk to change our room."

"You said this was the last one."

"Then we can go to another motel."

"By that time, there won't be anything left of the night."

"Sleep is overrated." What she meant was sleep would be impossible in the same bed with Cameron, but she'd be damned if she said that out loud. She could just picture his dark body lying against the white sheets, all bare-chested and sexy. Her breathing rate increased to the point she was panting.

"Sleep deprivation can have the same effects as drinking."

She had to shake her head to clear the image of Cameron in the bed. "What are you talking about?"

"If you don't get enough sleep, your reflexes are slowed, you're likely to nod off at the wheel while driving, or even hallucinate."

"All that because of a little lost sleep?" She could get that with a lack of oxygen in her lungs if she hyperventilated thinking about a naked Cameron.

He nodded and swung the door closed. "Come on. It won't kill you to share a room with me for one night."

Jennie chewed on her lip, knowing full well one night with Cameron could undo all the forgetting she'd done in the past ten years. Though, if she were honest with herself, all those memories she'd pushed aside were never really forgotten, just dormant. Until now.

"I'll even let you get the first shower." Cameron's voice was low and persuasive.

Like a straw house in one puff of the wolf's breath, Jennie's willpower caved. "Okay. But only because I'm tired and I need the rest." Tired? Ha! Rest? In a pig's eye. With Cameron Morgan lying next to her on the bed, she'd be awake all night, thinking of all the things she shouldn't do with him. She turned to him and poked a finger into his chest. "You…can sleep in the chair." She motioned to the chair in the corner with the wooden armrests.

Cameron's lips twisted. "It's going to be a long night." He jerked his head toward the bathroom. "Could you get a move on? I'd like to close my eyes for a few."

Jennie clutched her toiletries to her chest and dived for the bathroom. Once the door was closed behind her, she leaned against it, her blood pounding against her ears. Guilt at making Cameron sleep in the chair swamped her. She was already struggling with being alone in the same room with Cameron. Sleeping in the same bed would be…sheesh. Who was she kidding? Her traitorous body craved his touch and jerked in response to every unintentional contact.

Twisting the shower faucet on, she adjusted the temperature to hot, then readjusted it to cool. After hanging her dusty clothing on the back of the door, she slid behind the shower curtain and let the cool water soothe her heated skin. She tried not to think about how naked she was while on the other side of the door was the man who'd dominated her thoughts since she was sixteen.

She scrubbed her hair and skin and stepped out of the shower to dry off. With a towel wrapped around her middle, she stared at her dusty clothes, hating the thought of sleeping between clean sheets in them. But it couldn't be helped. She refused to sleep naked with Cameron in the room. Lathering her hands with hand soap, she scrubbed her bra and panties and hung them to dry on the door hook. Going commando, she slipped into her jeans and shirt, combed her hands through her hair and stepped out of the bathroom, before she could change her mind.

"That was quick." Cameron released the curtain at the window and moved across the floor. "I'll only be a minute. You know the drill. Don't let anyone in, stay away from the door and don't answer the telephone if it rings."

"Got it."

"Good." He stepped through the bathroom door and closed it behind him.

Jennie grabbed her cell phone and dialed home. As she waited for the ring tone, she glanced at the clock. One o'clock in the morning. Only a few hours until dawn.

"Hello?" Ms. Blainey answered the phone, her voice cracking with sleep.

"Ms. Blainey, this is Jennie."

"Jennie, honey, where are you?"

"We're staying the night in Denver." She heard the water start and squashed the image of a naked Cameron stepping beneath the shower. "Are you coming to the hospital in the morning?"

"Wild horses couldn't keep me away. I'd have come tonight, but they wouldn't let me in."

"No, they wouldn't." She'd always suspected that Ms. Blainey had a thing for her father and her concern for him made her that much more endearing to Jennie. Her father deserved some happiness in his life. If only he'd see Ms. Blainey as someone more than the house-keeper. "Could you grab some clean clothes for me when you come to town?"

"Sure, sweetie. Anything in particular?"

"Just what I normally wear is fine." She wasn't trying to impress anyone, especially not a bodyguard.

"Are you okay?" Ms. Blainey asked.

"Yes. I'm fine." She didn't want to go into detail about their run-in with the drive-by shooter. No use scaring the woman more than she already was. After saying her goodbyes, Jennie pulled the sheets back and glanced down at the jeans she'd ridden bareback in earlier that day. They had a layer of dust and the scent of horse all over them. Her mother had taught her to go to bed clean. The only way she'd sleep in jeans this dirty was if she were sleeping under the stars with the other livestock, not in a clean bed.

The sound of running water reassured her that she had a few minutes before Cameron came out of the bathroom. Jennie slid the jeans off and climbed between the sheets in nothing but her shirt and even that wasn't pristine or resembling anything nearly like clean. But she had to draw the line somewhere.

With Cameron sleeping in the chair and her body covered by the blankets, she shouldn't be worried or excited, or sensually aware of her nakedness beneath the sheets.

But she was.

When the water shut off in the bathroom, Jennie's breath caught in her throat. She switched the bedside light off and rolled to her side, scooting to the far side of the bed, away from the bathroom door and the spare chair. Then she squeezed her eyes shut, feigning sleep.

A moment later, the bathroom door opened, bringing with it a rush of warm, steamy air to wrap around her senses. The smell of soap and a male body wafted over her. She didn't have to open her eyes to know Cameron stood next to the bed in front of the chair he'd sleep in.

He leaned over the bed and plucked the pillow from beside her.

Jennie tried hard not to inhale his musky scent, but she couldn't hold her breath all night. She breathed in and wished she hadn't. She told herself that her physical reaction to Cameron was nothing more than the aftereffects of the danger they'd experienced earlier. A little voice in the back of her head screamed, *Liar!* She wanted Cameron as much, if not more, than when they'd been kids playing at making love.

She could hear him moving about the room, crossing to the window, probably peering out to see if there were any strange cars in the parking lot or people scurrying around, ready to attack them at any moment.

An involuntary reflex jerked Jennie's eye open. Okay, so she wanted a peek at him. When she focused in on him, she wished she'd kept her eyes closed.

Cameron stood at the window in nothing more than a towel. Light from the bathroom bathed him in a dark, golden glow. At six foot three, he filled the tiny room. His skin stretched tight over broad shoulders, tanned a rich brown from hours in the sun. Muscles rippled across his back, angling downward to a narrow waist visible above the white towel. Thick, brawny thighs strained against the towel wrapped around his waist and bulging at his firm buttocks.

Heat flooded through Jennie's body and she fought not to gasp aloud.

Why couldn't Cameron Morgan have gone to flab

in the past ten years? Instead, he'd improved with age. Damn.

He glanced her way and caught her staring. A grin spread across his face. "I thought you were asleep."

"Yeah, right." She flipped to her other side and punched the pillow beneath her chin. As if she could sleep when he was wearing next to nothing and so was she.

Cameron moved around the room and leaned over the chair, adjusting the pillow. When he settled on the seat, he stared across at her and frowned. "Get some sleep. I won't touch you."

"Good, because I don't want you to." Jennie closed her eyes, but the image of Cameron sitting in that hard chair in his towel was engraved in her mind. Eyes opened or closed, she'd see him. She chose to open her eyes.

He'd closed his eyes, but he was sitting up straight. The chair didn't have a headrest or any place for a tall man to lean his head.

Guilt swelled inside Jennie. Cameron had done so much for her, including saving her life on more than one occasion in the past two days. And she repaid him like this? After chewing on her lip for a full minute, she sighed. "Okay, you can sleep in the bed." She pulled the sheet back just enough for him to get in, but not enough to display her nakedness. He didn't have to know as long as she stayed on her side of the bed.

Cameron's eyes opened and he leveled a long look at her. "Are you sure?"

"Yes, just don't get any ideas. You're my bodyguard, nothing more. Don't touch me."

He raised his hand, scout-style. "You have my word. I won't touch you unless you want me to."

Jennie frowned. She hated it when he put it back on her. "Then there won't be a problem. I don't want you to touch me."

As soon as Cameron settled between the sheets, Jennie knew she'd made a huge mistake. The man had always been big, thus his success as a football player in high school. In a double bed, he practically filled the mattress without her on it.

Huddled all the way over to the edge, she could still feel his heat and smell his clean, musky scent.

When he turned his back to her, his towel-clad hip bumped into her naked one.

Jennie fought to keep from leaping out of the bed. She didn't want him to have any clue that his presence affected her and just how so.

"Are you okay?" he asked.

"I'm fine," she said through gritted teeth.

His chuckle shook the bed. "You don't sound fine."

Anger surged through her and she turned over to face his back. "I'm fine, so leave it, will you?"

"You're lying." When he rolled over to face her, his eyes were level with hers and he stared at her, all serious, the humor wiped from his lips. "You feel it, too, don't you?"

"Feel what?" Her words were supposed to be flippant, not breathy. What was wrong with her?

"The heat, the energy. Like it used to be."

"Nothing's like it used to be." If anything, the intensity was even greater than when they were kids. "We're not the same people."

His smile faded and he reached out to run his thumb over her scarred eyebrow. "I know."

Jennie melted at the warmth of the feathery touch. "You promised not to touch me."

His thumb jerked away from her face, his hand hovering beside her cheek. "I'm sorry. It's just so hard to be this close and not touch."

Caught in his gaze, she hesitated and then like a bee drawn to honey, Jennie leaned her face into his palm. "Yes, it is."

Cameron's fingers curled around her jaw and slid up into her hair, twisting around the strands and tugging her closer, until his lips hovered over hers. "I take it you want me to touch you."

Staring into his deep emerald gaze, Jennie couldn't form enough thought to articulate an answer. She nodded. When he leaned forward to claim her lips, panic set in. "Cameron?"

"Yes, Jennie?" he breathed against her mouth.

She swiped her tongue across suddenly dry lips. "Are you ever afraid?"

"When it comes to you, sweetheart, I'm shakin' in my boots."

"You aren't wearing boots." The way he said *sweetheart* turned her inside out. With only a couple hours left of the night, she wanted more of this man than to lie next to him and sleep. No matter how scared she was at reopening their relationship, she couldn't lie next to him without touching him. "Are you going to talk all night, or are you going to kiss me?" Jennie braced herself for his kiss. No amount of preparation could have kept that kiss from rocking her world.

CAMERON LAY NEXT to Jennie wondering what he'd done right in his life to deserve a second chance with this woman. As much as he wanted to touch her, hold her and make love to her, he was afraid. More afraid than when he'd had a dozen rifles pointed at his chest in a jungle in Africa.

Looking back, he'd been selfish by leaving Jennie. If he'd dug a little deeper, he might have found out about her father's heart condition. He might have saved her from an abusive marriage. He regretted that most. Had he not run away from his family and Jennie, he might have saved a lot of people from heartache.

Every time he glanced at the scar over her eye, Cameron wondered what other scars the bastard had left on Jennie. The knot in his belly tightened. He blamed himself for not being there for her.

As Cameron hesitated in the descent to kiss her lips, Jennie's eyebrows dipped to the middle, wrinkling her forehead. She reached up, her hands circling the back of his neck, and she brought him down to her.

For such a tough woman who could outride, outwrangle and mend fences better than most men, her lips were as soft as the petal of a rose, her skin as smooth as silk.

Cameron sank into her, drinking her in like a thirsty man. His mouth slanted over hers, his tongue delving between her teeth to taste her. As he gathered her into his arms and held her body close to his, he thanked his lucky stars he'd taken this job, because who else could he trust to look out for her?

Long, firm fingers slid over his shoulders and down his sides. He liked the callouses on her hands, callouses that spoke of hard work and dedication to a belief in family and tradition.

Her movements stirred his blood, making it race south to tent the towel barely covering the lower half of his body. His own shaking fingers worked the buttons of her shirt, fumbling each tiny button through the hole, working his way down the front to the last one.

One of her feet slid up his calf and soon her naked thigh was lying across his. When he realized she wasn't wearing anything but the shirt, his hands stilled and he stared down into her face, visible from the bathroom light shining into the bedroom. "Do you know where you're going?"

"I know exactly." Her hand slid down over his buttocks and she pulled him to her, his rigid erection pushing against terry cloth into the soft skin of her belly. "If we don't hurry, we won't get there before we have to leave." She sat up and shrugged out of the shirt, exposing every inch of her flesh to his view. Then she reached out to tug off the towel.

Cameron shifted until the towel slipped from beneath him.

With a sigh, Jennie tossed the towel to the corner.

As the light kissed her body with a gentle golden glow from behind, Cameron's breath caught in his throat. If anything, she'd become more beautiful over the past ten years, her body swelling into full womanly curves, stretched taut and sinewy from life on the ranch.

She moved over him with the grace of a cat, straddling his hips and pressing her body down over him, fitting herself to him like a glove.

He let her have the lead, his fingers gently stroking her back. If she wanted to take this further, she could. She could stop any time. He wouldn't force her.

With a fervent prayer to the heavens, he pleaded that she wouldn't stop, because if she did, he would be in a world of hurt.

As she leaned over, her lips hovering above his, Jennie's breasts pressed against him, a light teasing touch, with the firm tips twisting into the hairs on his chest.

His big hands glided over her back and down to the swell of her hips, his erection poised against her opening. "What about protection?"

Her eyes widened and she leaned up on her hands, the movement pressing him into her. "Do you have anything?"

"I don't know." He lifted her off him and laid her on the bed beside him. Then he climbed out of the sheets. "Let me check in my wallet." As he strode into the bathroom where he'd hung his jeans on the back of the door, he wondered if by the time he returned, she'd change her mind.

Despite the fires raging inside him, he knew it was better if she decided against taking the next step— better for her. Perhaps this reprieve was all she needed.

He found a foil package inside his wallet, buried beneath his credit card. When he returned to the room, he fully expected her to be lying with the sheets up to her chin and telling him she'd made a mistake.

Instead, he found her on her side, her cheeks blooming with color and a shy but sexy smile on her face. She held out her hand. "Give it to me." She took the package from him and grabbed his hand, pulling him back onto the bed.

Once he was lying next to her, she kissed his lips and trailed a line of kisses down his chin to his neck, where she nibbled the base of his throat. As her lips scorched a path down his torso, his body reheated to the boiling point, his member jutting to attention.

By the time she slid the condom down over him, she

wore a light sheen of perspiration, the moisture catching the light and making her glow softly.

Then she lay down next to him and pulled him on top of her.

At that point, Cameron could no longer be passive; he bent to kiss her, sliding into her at the same time, stretching her inner walls with his size. He stilled, afraid he'd hurt her, she was so tight.

Her hands clutched his buttocks and she pulled him deeper.

He settled into long steady strokes, moving in and out of her, the speed increasing the closer he moved to climax.

Jennie's knees rose, and she planted her heels in the mattress, rising to meet him with each thrust, her passion evident in the way her back arched off the bed and the sexy moans escaping her lips.

As he reached the peak and plummeted over the edge, he heard her cry out his name. He collapsed over her and rolled to the side, holding her against him, the connection unbroken.

When he could think again, he felt her shoulders shaking and the moisture against his chest where her face pressed into him. Jennie was crying.

What had he done? "Jennie? Are you all right?"

She held on to him and buried her face deeper into him, refusing to respond to his quiet entreaty.

He tried to push her away enough to see down into her eyes, but she clung to him, the tears continuing to flow. "Why are you crying?"

"I don't know." She sniffed and rubbed her hand across her wet cheek. "I never cry."

Maybe she needed to do it more often. "You don't have to be strong all the time, you know."

"Yes, I do."

"Let me be strong for you."

She pulled back enough to look up into his eyes. "And when you leave?" Tears trembled on the edges of her eyelids, and she dashed them away.

When he left? Cameron hadn't thought that far ahead.

"No, don't bother answering. I'll take what I can get for the moment. After this whole thing dies down, I don't want anything else from you."

That hurt. Like a kick in the gut. She didn't expect anything from him, because he'd only disappoint her. That's the message Cameron read loud and clear.

For that matter, what were his intentions where Jennie was concerned? "I'm not going anywhere." There, he'd said it. Was this what he wanted? To stay with Jennie forever? To live on the Flying W next to his family's ranch and continue with the same old feud?

If it meant he could be with Jennie…yes.

Cameron gathered her closer, wrapping his arms around her. He couldn't let her go. He was falling for her all over again.

After a while her body relaxed against him and her breathing became more rhythmic. She'd fallen asleep.

Not Cameron. He had too much to think about— tonight's attack, the barn burning, the shots taken at Hank. He had to lay out a plan to get Jennie through another day alive.

For a moment, his eyes closed, exhaustion pulling at him until he gave in and dozed.

A sharp buzzing tone woke him. He glanced at the

door and the window. Nothing moved. Then the buzzing tone sounded again.

Jennie stirred in his arms. "Are you going to answer that?"

He didn't want to let her go, but he laid her to the side and climbed out of the bed. The cell phone was in the bathroom with his jeans and wallet.

Cameron strode naked across the room and reached the phone as it buzzed again. He flipped it open, noting the number to the office. "Yeah."

"Cameron? This is Lenny. I found something."

Cameron glanced at his watch on the counter. Two-thirty. "Don't you ever sleep, Lenny?"

"Not when I'm on to something."

"What do you have?"

"Scoop on two of the four persons you wanted me to check into."

"Important stuff?"

"Can't tell. You'll have to decide if it's relevant."

"Then why the call at two-thirty in the morning?"

"I hacked into Vance's Internet blog and found a picture of Vance Franklin and a couple of his buddies."

"Buddies? So, the man had friends, how does that connect them to what's been going on at the Flying W?"

Lenny continued, his sentences short and excited, "I almost didn't think much of it, until I recognized one of them."

He had Cameron's attention now. "Who?"

"Milo Kardascian."

"Kardascian, as in the dead CEO?" He switched the phone to the other ear.

"Yeah, the one up to his eyeteeth in debt to the

Russian mafia." Cameron could hear Lenny take a long breath as if he'd run out of air. "And get this…"

Cameron waited, not wanting to interrupt the man.

"They're all standing in front of a casino. If I'm not mistaken that casino is in Central City."

"Gambling buddies," Cameron said quietly. "Any ID on the other guy?"

"Not yet."

"I'd like to get a look at that picture. He could be the one who killed Vance."

"Could be." Lenny yawned into the phone. "Geez, what time is it anyway. Holy smokes it's way past midnight. I'm beat. I'm about to head out the door. You want me to bring you what I have?"

"No. Not with all the shooting that happened earlier. It's not safe."

A clearly distinct snort sounded in Cameron's ear. "Look, I'm an agent in this firm, too. I can stand a little heat. Besides, they're not looking for me or following me."

Lenny's expertise wasn't in shooting, fighting or bodyguarding. His talent was digging into computer systems to find valuable information. But just like most guys, he wanted to be involved in the more glamorous aspects of the bodyguard business.

What would it hurt to let him bring the picture and information to them? Besides a picture was worth a thousand words and Cameron wanted to see who this gambling partner was. Would he be someone they recognized? Someone close to the Wards or Morgans? Could there be a snake hiding among them and they didn't know about it? The thought sent chills across his skin. What if one of the Ward ranch hands was involved in the attempted murders? Or maybe the new man at the Morgan ranch. Had the Morgans been harboring a killer? Was Cameron's own family in danger?

"Okay. Bring it to—" Cameron gave him the address and directions to the twenty-four-hour convenience store next to the hotel. "I'll be watching for you. Whatever you do, stay in your car."

"Don't worry." Lenny laughed. "I'm sure there's nothing more dangerous to worry about than a few drunk drivers on the road. I'll be there in a few."

Cameron hoped Lenny was right.

Chapter Fourteen

Jennie had heard only half of what Cameron was
talking about in the bathroom. When he walked back
into the bedroom, she sat up, pressing the sheet to her
breasts and pushing the fog from her brain.

Still shirtless, Cameron zipped his jeans, leaving the
top button undone—a deadly combination.

"Who was on the phone?" she asked.

"Lenny." Cameron shoved his cell phone into his
pocket. "He found an online photo of Vance Franklin's
gambling buddies." Cameron's gaze seared a path
across her exposed skin. "Ever heard of Milo Kardascian?"

Jennie tried to think back over all the people she'd
run into while married to Vance and that name didn't
touch on any memories. "I'm better with faces."

"Milo Kardascian was the first CEO murdered. He
was also in over his head in debt to the Russian mob."

"Sounds like a great guy." She shook her head. "You
say Lenny found a picture of Vance with this guy?"

"Yeah. There's another man in the picture Lenny
didn't recognize. He's bringing it by on his way home."

"You sure that's a good idea?" Jennie scooted to the

edge of the bed, pulling the sheet around her. Why was she so shy about being naked around Cameron after what they'd just shared? A more confident woman would strut across the floor naked and to hell with clothes.

The sad fact was that while she could hold her own on a horse, Jennie lacked confidence about her femininity. Part of the blame fell squarely at her ex-husband's feet. On more than one occasion, he'd called her frigid and boring in bed. Words that hurtful were hard to forget. She wondered what Cameron's impression had been? Was he bored by her performance?

She shook the thought from her mind, grabbed her shirt and jeans from the floor and dived for the bathroom. Before she got there, Cameron moved in front of her, blocking her path.

"What happened between us was no accident and no mistake."

Her face flamed. Had the man also developed an ability to read her mind? "Don't worry, I'm not staking a claim. We only had sex, nothing more." Burning with embarrassment, she tried to duck around him.

His hand shot out to capture her around the waist. "Now who's running?"

"I am." She shook his hand loose and made it to the bathroom before he could stop her again. With the door shut and locked behind her, she collapsed against its cool paint.

"I'm going to meet Lenny at the convenience store next to the motel," Cameron called through the door. "Stay here."

Panic gripped her. That feeling, as if something bad was about to happen, welled up inside her and threatened to clog her throat. "I want to go with you."

"No, it's best if you stay inside. The less people who see you, the better."

She struggled to slide her legs into her jeans. "No. I want to go with you." The shirt twisted as she tried to get her arms into it. Then she heard the sound of the door to the room closing.

He'd left her.

Her hands shook when she twisted the bathroom door handle. It didn't open. She took a full five seconds to comprehend it didn't open because she'd locked it. Five wasted seconds she could have been running after Cameron.

As she raced across the floor, she buttoned her shirt and zipped her jeans. Still barefoot, her fevered gaze searched the room for her boots, fear rising in her like floodwater.

Something bad was going to happen. She could feel it. One boot was beneath the chair, the other took a little longer to find beneath the bed, buried in the blanket that had slipped off during their lovemaking.

Jennie hopped across the room, pulling her boots on as she went. When she reached the door, her hand froze.

Cameron had told her to stay put. If she went out now, he'd be distracted by her presence. She raced through the room to turn off all the lights and ran back to the curtain to peer out.

Nothing moved in the parking lot below. The brightly lit sign for the combination gas station and convenience store shone through the branches of a tree. Only a few yards away. Surely nothing could happen in that short distance. The shadow of a very tall man slipped through the hedges between the motel and the convenience store. By the way he walked, it had to be Cameron.

Jennie grabbed her key card, took one last look through the curtain and ducked out the door, running for the stairwell. Careful not to make a noise, she eased down the concrete and metal steps to the ground, slipping past door after door of rooms with sleeping guests, blissfully unaware of the possible drama going on outside.

When she reached the hedges, she spent a few seconds looking for the point at which Cameron passed through what looked like a solid mass of branches. Then she was through and walking in the glare from the convenience store lights.

As she rounded the corner of the building, she noted two cars parked in front of the doorway. She didn't see any sign of Cameron and was about to step out front and into the building when a hand clamped over her mouth, an arm wrapping around her middle. Someone really strong had hold of her, dragging her back into the bushes.

Although she screamed into the palm, the sound was drowned out by the noise of traffic passing on the interstate. Her struggles did nothing to dislodge the arms or hand and she ceased her efforts, fighting the rising rush of panic.

Think, Jennie, think. All the lessons she'd learned about self-defense from her father couldn't have gone in one ear and out the other. Where were those reflexive actions she'd honed?

When the right move came to her, she braced her feet against the ground and prepared to jab an elbow into her adversary.

At the moment before she swung her arm, a voice hissed into her ear, "I thought I told you to stay put."

Jennie went weak with relief, collapsing against the muscled wall of Cameron's chest. Thank God.

His hand slipped from her mouth. "How am I supposed to keep you safe if you don't listen to my instructions?"

"I'm sorry. I had to know what was going on." She had to know he was all right.

"You'll only be in the way." His words were harsh, but his arms tightened around her. "You're a distraction, Jennie. And I mean that in a good way." He pressed a kiss to the side of her neck. "Now, go back to the room."

"I don't like you being out here where I can't tell what's going on."

"I don't like you being out here where someone can shoot you. Now go." His voice was firm with a touch of anger.

Jennie didn't blame him for being angry with her. He was the expert bodyguard, she was just the body to be guarded. "Okay. But I don't like it."

"I'll be there as soon as I get the packet from Lenny." He turned her in his arms and brushed the hair from her face. "I'll be back. I promise."

Jennie nodded, tears stinging her eyes. She turned to leave.

Before she could take two steps, Cameron pulled her into his arms, his body rigid. "Shh."

"What?"

He nodded toward the brightly lit gas pumps. "There's Lenny." He pushed her deeper beneath the branches. "Stay here."

Jennie crouched in the bushes, holding her breath, her gaze darting to the street, searching shadows. The red-haired techno geek from the agency unfolded his long, lean frame from a nondescript sedan just like the one Cameron borrowed from the agency. He plugged the gas pump nozzle into the car and glanced around casually.

Cameron stepped onto the concrete and moved slowly toward the convenience store, his hands tucked in his pockets, barely looking around.

When Lenny spotted Cameron, he nodded almost imperceptibly and continued pumping gas.

How was he going to pass a packet of information to Cameron without looking obvious about it? Jennie's gaze moved from Cameron to Lenny and back again. She pulled in a deep breath and let it out slowly in an effort to calm her leaping nerves.

As Cameron opened the glass door to the store, tires squealed in the street and the same beat-up car that had chased them earlier swerved into the gas station.

A flash of fire flew through the air toward the car Lenny was filling with gas.

Jennie leaped to her feet and shoved a fist into her mouth to stifle the scream rising up in her throat as she watched the scene unfold as if in a violent movie.

The flash of fire was a Molotov cocktail, a bottle filled with flammable fluid. When it hit the side of Lenny's vehicle, it exploded, spewing gas and fire everywhere.

Some of that fire landed on Lenny's sleeve and pants and he yelled out, patting the fire with his bare hands.

Cameron yelled out, "Run, Lenny!"

A gunshot rang out and the glass door behind Cameron shattered. Someone screamed inside.

Cameron dived behind a newspaper stand as bullets flew past him.

Lenny cried out, "I can't put it out!" He slapped at

the fire engulfing his legs and spreading up his torso, his face contorted in pain and fear.

"Run, Lenny! Get away from the car, now!" More bullets slammed against the windows behind Cameron. He tucked and rolled behind a car.

The vehicle lobbing the bullets and fire skidded sideways and raced around the gas pumps and out onto the road.

As Cameron's head appeared above the top of the vehicle, the world exploded in a thunderous roar and a huge ball of fire.

Jennie was knocked off her feet, falling back into the bushes, her ears ringing, her vision temporarily blinded by the intensity of the flash.

When the bright ball of light faded from her eyesight, Jennie could see smoke and fire billowing from the crater where Lenny's car had stood—no car, no Lenny.

Scrambling to her feet, she ran across the parking lot to the car behind which Cameron had taken cover. He was just sitting up.

Jennie hooked an arm around his waist and hauled him the rest of the way to his feet. "Get up!" She had no idea whether or not the other gas lines would explode and she didn't want to wait around to find out. With all the strength she could muster, she dragged Cameron around the back of the building. Not until she had solid brick and mortar between them, did she let go.

Cameron dropped to his knees and clutched his head in his hands. "Lenny?"

Shock set in and Jennie clamped her hands on her arms, rocking back and forth to keep her knees from banging together. "I'm sorry, Cameron, I didn't see him." What she'd just witnessed was a scene from a war zone, not a quiet city street in Denver. That and the death of a gentle man destroyed her faith in normalcy. She turned around and took a step.

"No. You stay put." Cameron's hand clamped on her arm. "I'll go look. I need to check on the people who were inside the store, as well."

She'd only been worried about getting him out of the way of further explosions, not the rest of the world.

Cameron pushed to his feet and staggered a few steps before he straightened. "Stay behind the building." When she opened her mouth to protest, he pressed his fingers to her lips. "Don't argue with me on this. I need to know you're safe."

When he removed his fingers, she grabbed his hand. "And I don't need the same? What if another tank explodes?"

"If I can help anyone, I have to."

"Go then, but I'm going, too." Her back straightened and she clamped her jaw tight to keep her teeth from chattering. If he stepped around the building and another explosion occurred, he could die. If that happened, she wanted to die with him.

Cameron shook his head, closed his fingers around hers and moved to the edge of the building. "You're hardheaded. Did anyone ever tell you that?"

"A number of times." She peered around Cameron, scanning the street for the car and driver that caused all the chaos in front of them.

"Damn." Cameron dropped her hand and took off running toward a lump of what looked like burned rags lying on the concrete several yards away from the burning wreckage of Lenny's car.

He stopped and stared at the lump, then turned and bent at the waist and vomited. When he straightened, he turned a hollow-eyed look toward Jennie.

"Lenny?" she asked.

He nodded and strode toward the building. Jennie followed, refusing to look back at either the remains of Lenny or the fire that could cause another explosion at any second.

Up to this point, the only person who'd actually died in this scene was a person whose death Jennie had come to terms with well over nine years ago, her husband, Vance. With the image of Lenny's charred body indelibly etched into her memory, Jennie knew she couldn't let another person die trying to save her life. Especially not Cameron.

The windows that hadn't been shattered by bullets had blown in with the force of the gas tank explosion. Lying amidst shattered glass and grocery items littering the floor were two men. The attendant and an unsuspecting customer caught in the cross fire.

After a quick check for pulses, Cameron took the shoulders and Jennie grabbed the heels of the first man they came to and they half dragged, half carried him out behind the building. They performed the same service for the other injured man, laying him down on the grass.

As Jennie applied pressure to a bleeding wound, the sound of sirens grew into a wailing scream. Police cars and fire engines pulled in close to the station, their bright lights strobing the night sky.

Cameron stood. "I'll let them know we have wounded back here. Will you be all right?"

"Do I have a choice?" Her lips twisted into more of

a grimace than a smile. How could she smile again knowing that someone wanted to kill her badly enough he'd killed another person who stood in the way?

Alone with the two injured men, Jennie allowed a few tears to escape and trickle down her dirty cheeks. A wave of self-pity washed over her. For a moment, she let it sink in, but when it threatened to pull her under, she squared her shoulders and went back to work. Lenny was dead and there was nothing she could do about it. She couldn't undo the damage and she couldn't trade places with the man.

BY THE TIME THE POLICE had taken their statements and the emergency personnel had loaded the injured and dead into ambulances, Cameron was exhausted— mentally and physically—and the sun had just slipped into the sky. He'd yet to call Evangeline and tell her about Lenny. What could she do at this point? Why lose sleep over something she couldn't change.

Lenny. The man wouldn't hurt a fly. For all his desire to be a field agent, he'd been too nice and too gullible to hack it in the tough situations that invariably arose in their line of work.

Cameron stopped himself from saying it aloud, but he couldn't help thinking he shouldn't have agreed for Lenny to meet him. If he'd just waited until morning, he could have gone to the agency and got the information from a tired, but still living Lenny.

He dug for the cell phone in his pocket and flipped it open. The screen was cracked, but the device re- mained functional. Without further hesitation, he hit the speed-dial number for Evangeline's personal line.

"Cameron? What time is it?" Her voice sounded

groggy as if he'd woken her from her sleep. "Are you in trouble?"

He had to swallow several times before he could speak. "There's been an explosion."

"Oh my God. Anyone hurt?" Her voice sharpened with no more traces of sleep. "Are you all right? How's Jennie Ward?"

"Jennie and I are fine." His chest squeezed so tight he felt as though he was having a heart attack. "It's Lenny."

"Lenny? What's wrong with Lenny?"

How else did you tell the boss one of her best employees and a good friend was dead? "He's dead."

For a long moment silence reigned on the other end of the line. Cameron thought he'd lost the connection and pulled the phone from his ear to check the display.

"What happened?"

When he finished an abbreviated version of what had happened, another long pause followed.

"Cameron?" Evangeline's voice shook.

"Yes, ma'am." His emotions raw with the same feelings he'd experienced in Somalia when he'd lost a member of his Special Forces team, he reverted to his military training. No time for sentiment, just get the job done.

"Find the bastard who did this."

"Yes, ma'am." He clicked the off button.

Jennie refused to be taken to the hospital in an ambulance and, for once, Cameron agreed. She let the emergency medical technicians check her over, and she insisted they tend to Cameron's cuts and scrapes, but when all was said and done, neither Cameron nor Jennie left in an ambulance.

"Come on, we have to get as far away from here as possible. If the guy who did this comes back, I don't want you in the line of fire."

"It's almost time to go to the hospital for my father's procedure." Jennie glanced down at the dirt and blood streaks that crisscrossed her arms and clothing. "Do we have time for a quick shower? I don't want to scare Ms. Blainey."

She was a dirty mess, but as far as Cameron was concerned, she was a beautiful dirty mess. He wanted to gather her in his arms and hold her until all the bad things that had happened in the last few hours went away.

"I'll stand guard and make sure you get that shower, if that's what you want."

"It is. Thank you." She stepped close to him and rocked up on her tiptoes. "Thank you for being here for me." Then she pressed a quick kiss to his lips before she dropped back on her heels and ducked through the bushes.

The softness of her lips against his filled him with a warmth he needed at just that moment. Cameron followed her through the hedge and into the motel room where he stood guard while Jennie had a shower.

Their opposition was playing rough. How much rougher would it get before they zeroed in on the guy and took him out? Hopefully, before anyone else got hurt.

Chapter Fifteen

Five hours later, they pulled away from the hospital and Jennie sighed. "Thank God, Dad's going to be okay. The stent they put in should hold him for a while. I hope the stress of this investigation doesn't cause him any more damage."

"The man's too stubborn to back out of a fight. He'll hold his own, just like his daughter. Must be where you get it." Cameron reached across the console and lifted her hand into his. "Tired?"

"Too tired to think." Leaning her head back against the headrest, she closed her eyes. She loved the way Cameron's large, rough hand held her smaller one. No matter what kind of work she did, from mucking stalls to castrating bull-calves, she could count on Cameron to remind her she was a woman all over.

He squeezed her hand and let go to negotiate a turn. "Are you too tired to stop by the Prescott Personal Securities offices?"

That perked her up. "Hell, no. If there's any chance we can get into the files or find the picture Lenny was looking at, we need to do that. The sooner the better."

"That's what I was thinking. I also have a gut feeling

that the man who's been shooting at us is someone we know—someone possibly close to our families."

Her glance shot his way. "You think so?"

Cameron stared straight ahead, both hands wrapped tightly around the steering wheel. "It would explain how someone got into the barn without notice, both to stash the snake and to burn it down."

"You think maybe he's someone who knew Vance?"

"Had to be. That would narrow the search down to anyone around ten years ago."

"The only person on the Flying W who doesn't meet that criteria is Rudy." That meant Doug, Stan and Ms. Blainey were suspects. Not that Jennie could ever accuse any one of them of murder. They were family. "What about the Bar M?"

"We've had a complete turnover in the past ten years except for our foreman and Ty Masters. Ty's out of commission with a broken leg and our foreman went back east to help his mother move into a nursing home."

"The guy could have known Vance since he left the Flying W. Heck, Cameron, he could be any of the new folks, too." A chill shook her from the top of her spine down to the base and it had nothing to do with the car's air-conditioning. All this talk about suspects had her scared.

"As far as I'm concerned, everyone is a suspect until we catch this guy."

"So far, this person has only gone after me and my father. Do you think he will turn on your family if he can't get to us?" Jennie thought of Emma, who'd come to see her when she'd stayed the night in the hospital, and of Molly, who'd been her friend despite the ongoing feud between the Morgan and Ward menfolk.

"We have to find that information. If he's someone we know…" From cold to hot, her blood boiled at the thought of someone she knew and trusted being the one who'd tossed the homemade bomb that killed Lenny. "Could you step on it?"

Despite the strain around the corners of his eyes, Cameron's lips tipped upward. "I thought you were tired."

"Not anymore." Jennie sat up straighter. "Let's find this guy before he hurts anyone else we care about."

When they entered the office just past noon, the place teemed with people, but none of them were laughing and joking like a normal office. A pall of silence hung over them.

Two people stood at the reception desk, two women as different as night and day. The younger one dressed all in black with her hair bottle-black and spiked. Her face was tinted a pasty white, her eyes lined in thick black. The other woman wore a pale gray business suit and had her light blond hair pulled back in a sophisticated French twist. When she spotted Cameron she stepped away from the reception desk and greeted him with her arms outstretched. "Cameron." She pulled him into a tight hug, her blue eyes glistening with unshed tears.

The younger woman in black stood like a child, not knowing what to do, a tear trembling on the edge of her ringed eyes. The tear slipped free and paved a smeared black trail down her pale cheek, bringing with it some of the thick makeup. Even her spiked hair seemed to droop.

Cameron noticed her and opened his arms to include her in the hug. "Come here, Angel."

As an outsider looking in, Jennie could feel the love these people had for their fallen teammate.

Others filed into the lobby and gathered around Cameron. The women cried and the men stood stoic, hiding their emotions beneath a thin, tough-guy layer. Each man and woman was an individual, but when it came to their team, they were one.

Jennie understood why Cameron liked his job. She could imagine that the camaraderie in the army had been much like this. Unlike the fighting and bickering that went on between the Bar M and the Flying W. All over a thirty-year-old misunderstanding between the two stubborn patriarchs. She couldn't blame Cameron for wanting to leave and be a part of something nobler. Hell, if she didn't have a job to do on the Flying W, she'd have leaped at the chance to be part of a bigger family. A family like Prescott Personal Securities.

Jennie faded back into a corner, giving the people of PPS their space to honor the fallen technology guru.

After several minutes of explanation and a quiet tribute to Lenny, they broke apart and went to their offices, leaving Cameron, Angel and Evangeline standing in the lobby.

Evangeline wiped the moisture from her cheeks, her lips straightening into a thin line. "I can't help going through all the 'if-onlys.'"

Cameron nodded. "I know. If only I hadn't agreed to meet Lenny at the gas station."

The older woman put a hand on his arm. "We can't blame ourselves. We didn't kill Lenny."

Cameron stared into Mrs. Prescott's eyes, his own narrowing. "That's right. We don't know if the guy who followed him wouldn't have killed him anyway. He tried really hard to kill Jennie and me, earlier."

"I saw your truck in the garage. We'll have it

repaired. I'm glad neither you nor Ms. Ward were injured."

Cameron looked around and spotted Jennie as if he just remembered she was in the room. He motioned her forward and cupped her elbow. "Evangeline, have you met Jennie?"

Clothed in the clean clothes Ms. Blainey had brought to the hospital early that morning, Jennie still felt dirty and gawky in front of this beautiful, classy woman. A stab of jealousy hit her in the midsection. How could Jennie Ward compete with a woman like Evangeline in Cameron's eyes? She rubbed her hand on her jeans before proffering it to Evangeline Prescott.

Mrs. Prescott brushed her hand to the side and engulfed Jennie in a bone-crunching hug. "I'm sorry you've had to go through so much."

The warmth the woman displayed following on the heels of the group mourning of Lenny almost made Jennie fall apart. A lump the size of a sock choked her throat and all she could do was hug the woman back. Any tinges of jealousy ebbed away with the woman's obvious care and concern for the people around her.

When Jennie finally had her emotions in check, she moved out of Evangeline's arms, her face heating. The woman was a stranger, and here the ranch girl had hugged her like a long-lost friend. Admittedly, she could use a friend right now and who better than the leader of such an elite organization? An organization that meant a lot to Cameron.

Evangeline hooked a hand around Cameron and Jennie's elbows and led them to her office with the floor-to-ceiling windows overlooking Denver and the surrounding mountains of the mile-high city. She left the door open and waved them to the bomber-jacket brown leather seats. "What's the plan of attack?"

Cameron sank into the chair as if he'd done it many times before. The man wasn't a bit on edge in the presence of his boss, which wordlessly spoke of a high level of mutual trust and respect between the two. "We need to get Cassie on Lenny's computer first thing. Lenny said he had information on the ranch hands and a picture of Vance's partner."

Evangeline wrapped her arms around her middle and nodded. "Cassie came in as soon as she heard the news. She's been digging through Lenny's files. I'm sure it won't be long before she has it for you."

"Good."

"Are you staying here until she gets it?" Evangeline asked.

Cameron shook his head. "I want to get back to the Bar M to make sure everything is all right with my family."

"Understandable." Evangeline turned to Jennie. "Are you going back to the hospital to be with your father?"

"No, I need to check on the stock. I'm sure there's a fence or two down somewhere."

Evangeline's gaze shot from Jennie to Cameron and back to Jennie. "Are you sure it's safe for you to be riding out in the open?"

Cameron stood, his lips pressed together in that stubborn line Jennie remembered so well. "That's what ranch hands are for."

She fought the urge to plant her hands on her hips in a combative stance, choosing to say in a soft, but determined voice, "It's my responsibility."

For a long moment Cameron stood silent, staring

down at her. When Jennie thought he'd argue, he inhaled a deep breath and let it out. "Let's get going."

Evangeline placed a hand on his arm. "Do you have an Internet connection out at the ranch?"

"Flying W has dial-up and the Bar M has satellite DSL." Cameron scribbled an e-mail address on a Post-it note and handed it to Evangeline.

"Good. We'll send a copy of the picture and what-ever else we find." Evangeline held out her hand to Jennie. "It was nice meeting you."

IN THE SEDATE SEDAN, Cameron drove most of the way to the Bar M Ranch without uttering a word. As if on a continuous feed, the image of the explosion replayed in his mind, over and over.

"You're thinking about Lenny, aren't you?" Jennie broke the silence as they neared the turnoff for Dry Wash.

"Yeah." The image of Lenny's charred body was a hard one to dispel from memory.

"You can't blame yourself, Cameron."

"I know that." He pinched the bridge of his nose between his fingers, pressure building inside him like a shaken carbonated beverage. He slammed his palm against the steering wheel. "Damn it all to hell! I shouldn't have let him come to meet me. I should have known it was too dangerous."

"Second-guessing won't bring him back." Jennie stared out the passenger window, the hollows under her eyes more pronounced due to her lack of sleep. "I thought maybe it was something I did that caused my mother to die. I worried that if only I had done something different, she might still be alive. But no amount of 'if-only' brought her back. It was just me and Dad."

Cameron remembered when her mother died after a short fight with lymphoma. That had been the only time the Morgans had shown up at a Ward function— at Louise Beatty Ward's funeral. The ten-year-old Jennie had been so small and fragile-looking standing with her hand in her father's, her face dry and pale. "I remember seeing you at your mother's funeral. It struck me funny that you didn't cry. Why?"

At first Cameron didn't think she'd respond to his question. She stared out her window, her face turned away from him. After a long pause, she shrugged. "Dad was pretty torn up about it. I had to be strong for him. I was the woman of the house with Mom gone." She laughed without any of her usual humor. "Ten years old and thinking I had to hold up the world."

"You always have." It was the same reason she'd stayed behind to care for her father. A strong sense of responsibility and family. Something he'd apparently been lacking.

"Yeah, except now." She shot a glance his way. "Now, I'm relying on you."

"Gripes your goat, doesn't it?"

She shrugged. "Not so bad."

"Your father is a strong man, even given his heart condition. Had he known you were holding back on your life because of him…"

A mirthless chuckle escaped her lips. "He'd have kicked my butt off the ranch so fast, I wouldn't have known what hit me."

They passed through the stone gate with the arching wrought-iron sign rising high above the road announcing the Bar M Ranch. "Are you sure I won't be in the way here? I could stay in the car while you see to business."

"You're coming in. My mother and sister would be hurt if you didn't."

"And your father and brother?"

"They won't say anything." Cameron's jaw tightened. "If they do I'll—"

"You'll do nothing." She sat up straighter as the car pulled into the drive leading around the sprawling ranch house. "I'm the one who doesn't belong."

He shifted the car into Park and grabbed for Jennie's nearest hand. "Jennie Ward, you've always belonged, and I won't let anyone say otherwise. If anything, I'm the one who doesn't belong."

"But you had the courage to leave and make a life of your own." She stared down at where their hands joined. "I see why you like working at Prescott. The people are great and they really seem to care about you."

"We all make choices for whatever reasons and they might be right at the time." He squeezed her hand. "That doesn't mean we can't make new choices when the time comes. Promise me we'll talk later?"

Emma and Molly Morgan stepped out on the porch and waved. Jack Sanders followed close behind, his gaze panning the immediate vicinity.

Jennie didn't answer. Her gaze focused on the women hurrying in their direction.

Was her silence her way of telling him they didn't have a future together? Was he willing to let her go this time without a fight? The muscles in his gut tightened. "Promise me, Jennie."

She turned to look at him, her face tired but resolute. "We'll talk."

Cameron released the breath he hadn't known he

was holding and got out of the car as his mother, Molly and Jack converged on them.

"Jack told us about the explosion." Emma threw her arms around Cameron and hugged him so hard he had to loosen her hold to breathe. "I'm so glad you're okay." She stepped back and laughed, brushing a tear from the corner of her eye. "I can't tell you how crazy this whole situation is making all of us. Your father and brother are carrying shotguns now every time they go out to check fences."

Molly hugged Jennie and smiled at her. "I'm glad you came with Cameron. How long has it been since I've seen you?"

Jennie smiled. "Since the last county livestock show before you started college."

Watching the easy way Jennie warmed up to his mother and sister made Cameron's anger rise at his father's and brother's dismissal of the Wards. How could they look at Jennie and not see what a wonderful individual she was, Ward or not?

"Got a call from Evangeline. Must have been while your cell was in a dead zone. She said something about finding the file you were looking for and sending it over the Internet."

Adrenaline leaped in his veins and he turned toward the house. Before he took a step, he looked back at Jack. "Could you stay out here?" He didn't add "to watch over the women." He didn't need to.

Jack got the message. "I'll cover. You go on."

As Cameron strode into the house, he cast one last glance at the three women. Molly and his mother were telling Jennie about the horse they'd been breaking, and Jack stood by, quietly watching over them.

"Oh, Cameron." His mother waved at him. "Our Internet service has been out since this morning. If you want to log on, you'll have to dial in."

"Damn." With the high-speed Internet down, it would take forever to log on much less download graphics. Cameron sighed and stepped into the cool interior of the home he'd grown up in.

"CAMERON SAID you lost all the tack and equipment in your barn." Emma Morgan shook her head. "What a waste."

"Yeah." Jennie had tried hard not to think about all they'd lost. She had enough to think about with someone trying to kill them. "That kind of equipment isn't something you buy overnight. It takes time to accumulate what you need."

Emma nodded. "Did you have insurance?"

"Yes, probably not enough. And until they pay, we have to do without. The utility and feed bills get paid first."

"Why don't you come see what you can use from our tack room?" Emma offered. "And then I'll show you the horse we got for Molly."

After all the years of feuding with the Morgans, Jennie frowned at Emma. "Why are you being nice to me? We're supposed to be mortal enemies."

Emma Morgan blew a strand of deep auburn hair out of her eyes. "Leave that up to the men, honey. They're the ones with the problem." Emma slipped a hand around Jennie's waist. "As for us girls, we like to get along with our neighbors, since they're so few and far between."

Jennie didn't argue with the woman and allowed her

to lead her toward the barn. Inside, Emma and Molly pulled out bridles, blankets and saddles Jennie could take to the Flying W for use until she could buy her own.

Their generosity caused an avalanche of emotions inside Jennie, rising up into a permanent lump in her throat. She had to swallow it every time she opened her mouth to speak.

With tears building around the corners of her eyes, Jennie laughed. "I don't know how we'll get all this over to the Flying W in the back of that little car."

"Don't worry about it. Molly and I can bring these out to you later today."

"And me," Jack added. He hefted the saddle to his shoulder.

"Don't you ride, Jack?" Jennie gathered a feed bucket filled with bridles and halters and followed him and Molly out of the barn.

"Sure. I have a ranch and horses. I used to ride all the time." He rubbed his empty hand down his leg. "Although, not as much with this old war injury."

Molly laughed and swatted at his shoulder as he set the saddle in the back of Emma's pickup. "Old, my fanny. Recent, more likely."

He grinned and dusted his hands on his jeans. "Okay, not so old. But it gives me grief in certain positions."

As Jennie dropped the bucket into the bed of the truck, she looked up at the sound of horses' hooves pounding toward them.

Jack spun toward the noise, his hand going to the pistol holstered beneath his arm.

Emma touched his arm. "Don't shoot. It's my husband and son."

Jack's hand fell to his hip and he relaxed.

Jennie didn't. She hadn't stood face-to-face with Tom or Logan Morgan since her mother's funeral. With her back straight and her wits on guard, she faced two of the men who'd made her and Cameron's lives hell ten years ago.

Tom Morgan led the way, galloping into the barnyard at full speed, bringing his horse to a skidding halt in front of the group standing there. His face was set in a grim line.

When he and Logan swung down from their saddles, Emma hurried to her husband. "What's wrong, Tom?"

He stared across at Jennie. "Fences are down between the Bar M and the Flying W."

Not again. Jennie shook her head. "Cut?"

Tom's lips tightened. "Yup." He turned to Emma. "Have you seen Brad?"

"Not for the past two hours."

"We need all the hands on the south fence as soon as possible."

"I'm coming." Jennie realized as she said it that she didn't have the means to follow them.

Jack stepped forward. "You can't go out there. It's not safe. It smells like a set up."

"I have to go. That fence is just as much a Ward fence as a Morgan fence. If the cattle crossed over I need to help move them back." Jennie laid a hand on Jack's arm. "I have to go. I only need a horse." She turned to Emma and Molly.

"I'd loan you a horse," Molly offered, "but are you sure you'll be all right out there?"

Jennie stared up into Tom Morgan's eyes and wondered the same thing. Other than the difference in eye color, Cameron could have been the spitting image of his father. "Yeah, I'll be all right."

Jack looked back toward the house. "I think we should tell Cameron. He'd want to go along with you."

"No time. We have to get the cattle back on the Flying W before they get mixed up in the Bar M herd."

Emma ran toward the barn. Jennie left Tom and Logan Morgan standing beside their horses and took off after Emma. With Ms. Blainey at the hospital with her father, there was no one at the Flying W ranch house to answer a call so she couldn't get word to her hands about the cattle. All she could do was go help the Morgans move the cattle back.

Emma had a horse tethered to a beam and was throwing a saddle blanket over it when Jennie entered the barn.

"Here, you finish saddling Danny Boy while I get a horse for me."

"You're not going, are you?" Jennie tossed a saddle over the horse's back, and flipped the stirrup up before she faced Emma.

"Of course I am. All hands are needed." She laughed. "I'm a hand just like anyone else."

Jennie's mother had never offered or been asked to ride out with the ranch hands. As far as Jennie could remember, she'd never seen her mother on a horse. Emma Morgan was more than willing and capable of riding out with the men.

In less than five minutes, the two women emerged from the barn and climbed into their saddles. Tom and Logan were already seated and Jack sat astride a four-wheeler. "You're not going anywhere without me."

Molly stood apart, biting a nail. "I'll stay here and

come with Cameron when he's done with the computer. Somebody needs to make sure he's all right."

"Good. Then go in right now, while we're still here." Jack waved her toward the house.

"I'm going. I'm going." She stared at her father, brother and mother. "Be careful, will ya?"

Jennie could see fear in the girl's eyes and the love of her family.

Tom Morgan's stern face softened. "Go on, girl. We'll be fine. Now get."

Molly smiled up at her father. "Keep an eye out for my friend, Jennie, won't you, Dad?"

He cast a quick glance at Jennie, completely free of any malevolence or spite. "We will."

Molly turned and ran to the house.

Afraid Cameron would stop her if he knew she was leaving the area without him, Jennie kicked Danny Boy's flanks and set off in the direction Tom and Logan Morgan had come.

Whoever was after them would get them by either shooting them or by sabotaging their livelihood. Either way, it would kill her father. Jennie had to get their affairs back in order before her father returned home. His heart couldn't take much more stress.

As she galloped away, she thought she heard a shout from the house. Jennie didn't turn back, refusing to stop to see if the shout came from an angry Cameron. This was something she had to do. He'd have to understand.

Chapter Sixteen

When Molly burst through the door of the ranch house, Cameron thought nothing of it. She always burst through doors. When she'd told him Jennie was about to ride off on a horse with his father, mother and brother, he'd hit the roof.

Standing on the porch and watching Jennie disappear over the ridgeline with the rest of his family almost killed him. He could only hope that between his father, Logan and Jack, they could protect Jennie and his mother. Cameron had to baby-sit the computer until the image of Vance's partner materialized through the dial-up line.

Why did the satellite Internet have to go down today of all days? The hourglass still showed the download was in progress at forty-five percent and that had taken a full ten minutes. By the time the download was complete, Jennie would be halfway across the ranch. Cameron paced the floor in front of the computer.

"Pacing won't make the computer move any faster, you know?"

"I know." He checked the job completion status. Forty-five percent. *Come on.*

Molly perched on the arm of a nearby chair and swung her boot-clad foot. "You love her still, don't you?"

"What do you mean?" He knew what she meant, but he didn't want to talk about it.

"You want to be with her."

"It's my job." *Job, hell.*

"Yeah, your job." Molly gave a very unladylike snort and stood. "You never got over her, did you?"

The computer screen switched to a screen saver of clown fish and coral. Cameron pounced on the mouse to bring the screen back to life. The download hourglass showed the operation still in motion. "Damn this system!"

With her arms crossed over her chest and a toe tapping on the wooden floor, Molly was the image of his mother. "You're avoiding my question."

Cameron cast a look out the window, wishing he'd see Jennie riding back into the yard. She didn't. "It's irrelevant. Drop it."

"No way, I'm on to something here. I think your feelings are very relevant to your pacing and temper and what's been wrong with you for the past ten years."

Cameron would have walked out of the room at that point if the hourglass hadn't disappeared. He clicked on the e-mail from Evangeline and then the JPEG attachment.

"Oh come on, brother. Admit it," Molly persisted in a quieter tone. "You still love Jennie."

Something inside of Cameron exploded and he turned to Molly, grabbing her shoulders. "Okay, I admit it. I love Jennie, always have. Right now I'm more afraid than I've ever been in my life. Will you let me be, so I can get this picture?"

"Okay, okay." Molly glanced around him. "Your picture is up."

Cameron dropped Molly's arms and spun toward the machine. Displayed on the screen was a full color photograph of three smiling men standing in front of a casino. The caption below read, Good times in Central City.

Out of all three faces, Cameron only recognized one. "Damn."

"What?" Molly leaned over Cameron's shoulder and stared at the picture. "Hey, that's Vance on the left and isn't the guy in the middle one of the ranch hands out at the Flying W?"

"Doug Sweeney," he confirmed.

"Yeah." Molly's eyes widened. "Who's the other guy?"

By the process of elimination, Cameron knew. "Milo Kardascian."

"So is Doug Sweeney the one who's been trying to kill the Wards? Their own ranch hand?" Molly rested a palm on Cameron's shoulder. "Holy cow."

"We don't know that, but he was Vance Franklin's gambling buddy and he knew Vance was still alive." Cameron stood so fast, the chair tipped over backward and crashed to the floor. "I need to get to Jennie with this."

"Wait, what else did it say?" Molly set the chair back on its legs and plopped into it, pulling up the text from the rest of Evangeline's e-mail. "Before you go, read this." She moved back far enough so Cameron could lean over her shoulder and read. "She says they didn't find anything on Brad Carter, not even a former address in Denver or Montana. But they found Doug Sweeney is in hock to several credit card companies. To the tune of fifty thousand dollars. Wow."

"No way a ranch hand can pay off that kind of debt."

"Unless he's hired to kill someone," Molly muttered under her breath, loud enough that Cameron still heard her.

The same thought had occurred to him. "Doug just doesn't strike me as a person who'd shoot someone in the back of the head."

"I'm sure that's what Ted Bundy's neighbors said about him." Molly leaned close to the screen. "Look here, there's a scanned copy of a newspaper clipping stating Lance Franklin and Ken Bennett of Bennett-Franklin Real Estate closed their doors to business due to bad investments and mismanagement of funds. Another clipping dated around that time claims gambling debts might have been the cause of the business going under."

"Sounds like our boy, Vance." Cameron couldn't believe Jennie had married the man and what hell he must have played with her life. Cameron's hands shook. If the guy wasn't already dead…

Molly read on, "They didn't get prison time because they couldn't find enough evidence to indicate the investments were a front." She clicked on another attachment. "This looks like Articles of Incorporation with the State of Colorado for a corporation whose president was Lance Franklin and whose vice president was another man, a Ken Bennett."

"Who the heck is Ken Bennett?"

Molly scanned the document and moved the cursor down. "Look at the date on the document."

Cameron leaned closer. "A little over a year ago."

He pulled out his cell phone and dialed the Prescott Personal Securities office. Thankfully, Angel wasn't the receptionist to answer and his call was properly directed to Evangeline.

"Cameron?" Evangeline's distinct voice came over the line. "Did you get the information I sent?"

"Got it. Have you found out anything more about this Ken Bennett?"

"Cassie just hacked into Ken Bennett's bank accounts and found a large sum of money deposited by Kingston Investments. A similar payment was made to Lance Franklin's accounts around the same time from the same investment company."

"The same Kingston Investments that manages the Kingston Trust?"

"That's right."

"So they sold their business to Kingston. Why am I not surprised?" Cameron shook his head. He was long past angry with this company. "Any idea what Ken looks like? Photographs? Anything?"

"Nothing yet." Evangeline paused for a second before adding, "One other thing. We're halfway through identifying the other coordinates on the disk, and you'll be interested to know fifty percent of them are owned by Tri Corp. Media, all purchased through Kingston Investment Group in the past two years."

"Sounds like the Kingston Trust might be a front for Tri Corp. Media?"

"That would be my bet." Evangeline's words were clipped. "Be careful will you? These people are playing for keeps. I don't want the same thing happening to you and your family as Lenny."

Cameron hung up without responding. He had to get to Jennie.

"Who is Tri Corp. Media?" Molly pinned him with her stare.

"Might be the corporation behind all this."

"So you think Doug is responsible for the attempts on Jennie's and her father's lives? Or do you think it's this Ken Bennett guy?"

"I don't know, but I'm not willing to take any more chances." Cameron hit the print key and waited for the picture of Doug to roll out of the printer. He had to get to Jennie before Doug did. If he was the one who'd killed Lenny, he wasn't getting any smarter and he was getting a whole lot more brash. How could he work with the Wards for so long and not let on to his true nature?

Cameron snatched the paper from the printer and spun about.

Molly stood in front of him. "I'm going with you."

His first instinct was to tell her no way in hell. A glance out the window at the empty yard and fields made him rethink his gut reaction. "Since there isn't anyone else here to watch over you, I guess you'll have to."

Cameron hurried to his father's gun safe, twirled the lock and maneuvered the combination until the safe clicked open. From inside, he removed a rifle and a pistol and loaded both with the shells in boxes lining a shelf inside the safe.

Molly's eyes widened. "I thought you didn't like to shoot because of your hands."

"I don't, but you're a good shot." He tossed the rifle to her and hefted the pistol into his own palm. "Let's go."

Outside in the barn, he took three minutes to catch, saddle and bridle a horse. Three minutes more than he wanted to spend. The entire time he saddled his horse, his brain churned on the information. Ken Bennett was the wild card. The unknown. The man was in real estate. Real estate.

After adjusting the girth he swung up on the saddle and turned to his sister.

Molly was right behind him. She was a natural in the saddle, just like his mother.

"What did Brad say about his former occupations?"

"Something about Montana and real estate."

Damn.

Cameron dug his heels into the horse's flanks and raced across the pasture and up over the hill headed toward the Flying W. He hoped like hell he wasn't too late.

JENNIE COULDN'T BELIEVE the amount of fencing down between the Flying W and the Bar M ranches. Stan and Rudy were already there rounding up some of the one hundred and fifty head of cattle that had wandered through the gap and spread out to graze on the other side.

"Where's Doug?" she asked.

Stan crooked his head to the side. "He was up by that bluff a few minutes ago, chasing a steer. Got cattle scattered all over the Bar M. It'll take all of us to get them back on the right side of the fence before they mingle with the Bar M herd."

"My cattle are on the other side of that ridge as its the only water source within a hundred acres, this side of the fence." Tom Morgan yanked his mount to a halt beside Jennie and turned in the saddle to point at the ridge behind them. "It might work best if we start from the ridge and work back this way."

Jennie smiled at the man who looked so much like Cameron. "Thanks, Mr. Morgan. Your help means a lot."

"Just want Ward cattle off the Bar M."

Emma Morgan reined her horse to a halt next to her husband and gave him a stern look. "Tom Morgan, play nice."

His jaw tightened for a moment.

When Emma's brows raised a notch, Tom's jaw relaxed. He turned his gaze to Jennie and stared at her for several moments. "You look like your mother." His voice was hard, almost accusatory.

Emma winked at Jennie. "Yes, she does."

Tom reached out to Emma and clasped her hand. "I once thought I loved Louise." He looked across at his wife. "Until an ornery redhead made me see the light." For the first time since Jennie had known Tom Morgan, he smiled. The same smile she recognized on Cameron's face when they were younger and not being chased by a crazed killer.

Emma squeezed her husband's hand and let go. "Are we going to round up some cattle or what?"

Tom's smile disappeared, a frown replacing it. "You're to stay with me."

Emma sat up straight. "You askin' or tellin'?"

Tom gave Jennie a sorrowful look and chuckled. "See what I mean about ornery?"

Jack Sanders eased close to the group on his four-wheeler. "I'm not liking this. There's way too much open space to keep you guys safe."

"We have cattle to deal with. They aren't branded and we have no other way of identifying them as Bar M or Flying W other than keeping them on the right side of the fence." Jennie shrugged. "Not much else we can do." Without waiting for Jack's protest, she wheeled her horse, swallowing the metallic tang of fear in her mouth. To Tom and Emma she called out, "I'll head up close to where Doug is and start moving cattle back this way." Then she ground her heels into the horse's flanks and took off at a gallop, half hoping Jack wouldn't follow. Part of her wanted his continued protection; the other part knew Jack's four-wheeler would only spook the cattle and make them more difficult to herd back to their own pastures.

Jack followed at a distance on the four-wheeler. Jennie moved amongst the trees, weaving in and out of the underbrush looking for strays. After a while, the engine noise ceased. When she looked back, she couldn't see Jack or the four-wheeler. Had he run out of gas, or had the engine quit?

A chill snaked its way down her spine and last night's shooting incident resurfaced in her memory. She glanced from side to side, imagining all kinds of bad guys lining up behind every tree. With a weak laugh she shook herself to dispel the image.

About that time, she spotted Doug Sweeney between the trees. She opened her mouth to shout a greeting and closed it again when she noticed he was piling branches onto something.

Doug reached behind him for another green branch torn from a nearby fir tree. When he moved, he revealed what he was attempting to hide beneath a layer of ever-green branches—a red-and-black four-wheeler, just like the one that had sped away from the clear mountain pool after someone dropped a dead goat into the crystal clear water.

Doug Sweeney, a man Jennie and her father had trusted for years, was the man sabotaging the ranch. Rage exploded inside so fast she didn't stop to think of consequences, she kicked her horse into a gallop and rode in between the trees and bushes and yanked her horse to a stop in front of Doug.

He turned to face her before she reached him, a rifle resting in his hands, aimed at her chest. "Stop there, Ms. Jennie."

"You!" That feeling of betrayal ratcheted her anger and the word came out as if she was spitting venom.

"Yeah, me." He hefted the gun in his hands. "Get down off that horse, Ms. Jennie."

Jennie ignored his command. Her horse, possibly sensing her changed mood, danced sideways. "How could you do this to my father? He trusted you."

His mouth tightened a moment before he said softly, "Call it survival. Now get down or I'll have to use this thing."

Jennie snorted. "Like you did last night?" Anger warred with her rising fear. How much more could she take? How many more attempts on her life and her father's before one took? Was this it?

"I don't know what you're talking about." He held the rifle steady.

"Don't play stupid with me. You're the one responsible for all the bullet holes in Cameron's truck and almost killing us in Denver last night."

He shook his head. "Sorry, you got the wrong guy. I was at a poker game with friends in Dry Wash. Got a couple witnesses who'd back me up." He lifted the rifle to his shoulder. "Get down."

She shifted in her saddle and braced her left foot in the stirrup. If she kept him talking, maybe the others would come looking for her. "At a poker game? If you didn't shoot at me and Cameron, who did?"

"Probably the same guy who killed Vance and shot

at your father the other day. Now get down, I'm kinda in a hurry."

With the pointy end of a gun aimed at her, Jennie gave a brief amount of thought to her options. If she spurred her horse, she might get away alive. Then again, she'd seen him shoot a deer in a perfect neck shot at two hundred yards. She sat on her horse not two yards from the business end of his weapon.

"If you didn't shoot at us, then why are you pointing a gun at me now?"

His gaze shifted to the four-wheeler.

"You're the one who put the dead goat into the pool." Her mind clicked away the other incidents. "And the snake?"

He nodded.

"The fences, including this one?"

His chin set in a stubborn line. "That was me, too."

"What about the missing cattle?"

"Sold to an auction to pay my poker debt." His brows rose and he reached out with one hand to grab her arm and drag her out of the saddle.

As she slid to the ground, Jennie asked, "Why? If you needed money, why didn't you ask?"

"It's more complicated than that." He turned the horse away from them and smacked him hard on the hindquarters. The gelding kicked up his heels and raced toward the Bar M barn.

As she watched her ride disappear over the hilltop, Jennie knew she was in trouble, yet something wasn't right with what Doug was saying. "What about the razor blade in my saddle?" Was Doug vicious enough to harm a horse?

The man shook his head. "I never wanted to hurt you

or your father. Vance stuck the razor blade in the saddle."

One more reason for Jennie to hate the man, as if she didn't already have enough to last a lifetime. "And you weren't responsible for the fire or Vance's death?"

"No."

Jennie stared hard at him. Was he lying? Her gut said no. Doug wasn't their killer or the man responsible for the attempts on their lives. Still… "Did you know Vance was alive all these years?"

Doug hesitated and then answered. "Yeah. He made me promise to keep my mouth shut."

"For ten years?"

"I owed him money for gambling."

"Blackmail?" Working side by side with a man living a lie made Jennie's stomach turn. To think her husband had been alive all this time. Had she known, she would never have let her guard down.

"Yeah, blackmail."

"Since Vance is dead and you didn't shoot at us, who did?" When Doug shrugged, Jennie lost control and shouted, "Tell me!"

"I did." A voice sounded from behind her. One she didn't recognize.

Jennie turned to stare at a man with sandy blond hair and blue eyes. He looked like the typical boy next door, except for the nine millimeter pistol in his hand.

"Who are you?" Jennie asked.

Doug held on to his rifle, now pointed at the man in front of him. "He goes by the name Brad Carter. He hired on with the Morgans as a front. His real name is—"

"I'll take it from here, Sweeney." He waved at Doug with the pistol.

"No way." Doug pushed Jennie aside and stood in front of Brad. "We can get them to sell without killin' anyone."

"Is that what this is all about? Selling the Flying W?" She stared from Brad back to Doug.

"There's a huge oil reserve in these parts," Doug said. "And people are willing to do anything to get to it."

"That's right, and you took too long." Brad nudged his horse closer. "The boss sent me out to finish the job you and Vance started."

"The boss can take a hike. I'm not doing this anymore." Doug stepped between Jennie and the stranger. "I didn't sign on for no killin'."

Brad's handsome face flushed red, his eyes widening. "What part of get rid of them didn't you understand? These people aren't going to leave their ranch on their own two feet." The more he said, the more his voice rose until he practically shouted. The man was clearly at the end of his tether.

Jennie's stomach roiled. She didn't like the way he talked to Doug as if she weren't there, as if she was already dead, and as if he might explode at any minute. With two guns within shooting range of her, she tamped down rising panic and mustered all the righteous indignation she could. "Damn right. We're not selling the Flying W and the Morgans aren't selling the Bar M, so get the hell out of here." While standing proud and firm, she used her peripheral vision to ascertain the distance between her and the nearest tree. About the length of a barn. If she ran, she might make it.

Doug nudged Jennie with his elbow. "Shut up, Ms. Jennie. He means business."

"I will not shut up." She brazenly shoved the tip of

his rifle away from her. "This land has been in our families for a century. We're not giving up so easily."

Brad waved his pistol. "Move, Sweeney."

"I won't let you kill anyone else like you did Vance." Doug stepped forward, raising his rifle. "Not that Vance didn't have it coming."

"Look, Sweeney, I don't have time for this." A loud bang exploded in Jennie's ears.

Doug Sweeney jerked backward, his eyes wide, his hand clutched to his chest where Brad's bullet had ripped a bright red hole through him.

Jennie stared in horror as Doug crumpled to the ground.

"Run." He called out on his last breath.

The one word galvanized her feet into action and Jennie turned to face the man on the horse.

The gun he'd used to shoot Doug was now pointed at her.

With no time to think through her options, she leaped toward the horse, flapping her hands.

Wild-eyed, the horse reared.

With one hand holding the pistol, Brad grappled with the reins and finally groped for the saddle horn, but he was too late.

The horse dumped his struggling rider on the ground. The handgun flew from his grip and landed a yard from him.

Jennie raced for the weapon.

As Brad reached for the pistol, Jennie stepped on his wrist with one hand and kicked the pistol with her other foot as hard as she could.

The pistol slid across the dirt into a tangle of brush and tall grasses.

Before she could breathe a sigh of relief, an arm clipped the back of her knees so hard, she fell face-first to the ground.

Brad flung himself over her, his heavy weight pressing her face into the ground, until she tasted grit and dirt.

"Bitch. You'll die for that."

Chapter Seventeen

Cameron had just topped a ridge and spotted his brother and other members of the Morgan family herding cattle out of the brush when the sound of a single gunshot echoed off the bluffs.

His horse danced around in a circle, emitting a nervous squeal. With a hard yank on the reins, Cameron spun his mount around.

"Was that gunfire?" Molly pulled alongside him, her horse breathing hard, sweat lathered on its neck and withers.

"Yes." Cameron's gut clenched. His gaze scanned the valley floor.

"Where did it come from?"

"Can't tell exactly, down there." He nodded at the view below. Had someone finally got to Jennie while he'd been playing around with the computer? Damn. He kicked his mount, plunging down the hillside into the long valley. His heartbeat thundered in his ears to the rhythm of the horse's hooves pounding against the earth.

Five people on horseback raced toward the bluffs on the far side of the valley. Cameron recognized his father, mother and brother. The other two were the foreman and the youngest of the Flying W ranch hands. A brief flash of concern made his breath catch in his throat, but the thought of Jennie dying due to a gunshot wound overrode his concern for his family.

His hands tightened on the reins and he pushed his horse faster, racing up beside his father. "Where's Jennie?"

Over the sound of horses' thundering hooves, Cameron heard his father shout, "Near the bluff."

"Where's Jack?" As soon as the question came out of Cameron's mouth, he spotted an abandoned four-wheeler. Half a mile farther ahead he could see a man running across a meadow. Jack Sanders.

Cameron urged his horse faster until he pulled up beside Jack.

The man was breathing hard, his breaths coming in shallow gasps. "Jennie disappeared behind that outcropping a few minutes ago and that's where the gunshots came from." He doubled over and sucked in a deep gulp of air. "Go! But be careful."

As the seven riders neared the stand of huge boulders and fir trees, a single horse rode out in a slow, steady pace. On its back sat the Bar M ranch hand, Brad Carter. Seated on the saddle in front of him was Jennie, a nine-millimeter pistol pressed against her carotid artery.

All seven riders pulled back on their reins as if in unison and waited for Brad's demand.

"I'll kill her if you don't back up and let me through."

Cameron's hands twitched, his thoughts going to the pistol in his belt and the rifle he'd handed to his sister, Molly.

As if reading Cameron's mind, Brad called out, "On

second thought, everyone drop your guns to the ground nice and easy and get off your horses."

Jennie squirmed against the arm clamped around her middle. "Don't do it. He's going to kill me anyway."

Cameron could see the flash of fear in Jennie's eyes and he fought to control the burst of anger. "Do as he says. Put your weapons on the ground." Cameron reached for the gun in his belt. When it came time to drop the pistol he'd brought along, he hesitated, Jennie's words echoing in his mind. If Brad planned to kill Jennie anyway, what good would it be to surrender their weapons?

Cameron swung out of his saddle, dropping to the ground. Instead of tossing his pistol to the side, he aimed it the best he could, cursing the way his hands shook. "Let her go, Ken."

The man's eyes widened. "H-how did you know?"

"The gig is up." Cameron moved closer. "It was all too convenient, Ty breaking his leg and you coming on board at the Bar M only a few weeks ago. That's when all the trouble began. What did you do? Set a trip wire for Ty's horse?"

"What's it to you?" Ken pressed the gun into Jennie's skin. "I've got the girl, so back off."

"We know you're the one who tried to kill us," Jennie said. "You've already killed Vance and Doug. You don't have an alibi and there are witnesses. We'll go to the police and they'll have you up on murder charges."

"I had to kill them." The gun Ken held to Jennie's neck shook violently. "If I didn't they'd kill me."

"I'll kill you if you don't let Jennie go." Cameron's jaw set in a hard line.

Ken Bennett's breath came in shallow gasps as if he was about to hyperventilate. He jerked the reins, and the horse pivoted until Jennie sat between himself and Cameron. "Shoot me and you'll be shooting her."

Jennie's eyes glistened with tears. "Do it, Cameron. Shoot me to keep this man from killing anyone else."

"No, Cameron, don't." Tom Morgan swung his leg over the saddle and dropped to the ground beside his son. "Brad—Ken, you won't get away. There are seven of us and only one of you. You'll have to go through all of us to get out of this jam. Give yourself up."

Cameron stepped forward and stood beside his father, for the first time in years in agreement. "My father is right. You won't make it out. You might as well give up."

"What you don't understand is that I can't." His voice cracked. "Even if I wanted to, I can't."

"Why not?" Cameron inched closer. "No one controls you. You're the only one who can control your own actions."

He snorted. "You don't know what you're up against. If I were you, I'd sell and get the hell out before anyone else dies."

"No one's going to sell. Even if we wanted to, there's been too much happening here for any deals to go through. The court will have it so tied up, it wouldn't sell for years. And no one else is going to die." Emma Morgan sat tall and proud on her horse. "Let the girl go and we'll let you through, no questions asked. Just leave the Bar M and our friends at the Flying W alone."

Ken shook his head. "You don't see, do you?" His voice and movements grew jerkier and more erratic. The wild look in his eyes was that of a desperate man. "These people suck the life out of you. If you don't give them what they want, you're gone. Even if you give them what they want, they'll still kill you."

Cameron's hand with the gun dropped to his side. "No one here is going to shoot you as long as you don't hurt us. And that includes Jennie. What people are you talking about, Ken?"

"The ones who want the oil." His voice cracked. "They take your money and blackmail you to do what they want." He laughed, no humor in the tone. "I'm a freakin' dead man."

"We can't help you if you don't let us. Tell us who's involved."

"I only have the name of one other investor. But then you probably already knew that."

"Who is he?"

Ken shook his head, his hand loosening from around Jennie's middle. "You're so good at figuring things out, look for it."

Jennie's face set in a grim line and her body slowly tensed.

Cameron knew that look. She was about to try something. He held his breath and prayed for the first time in years.

Then Jennie jammed her elbow into Ken's gut. At the same time she reached out and twisted the horse's ear. The big animal screamed and reared.

As if in slow motion, Ken and Jennie slid from the saddle.

The gun in Ken's hand discharged in a powerful bang.

Cameron ran toward the horse, snatching at the reins and moving it away from where Jennie lay against the rocky ground. With the horse out of the way, he could see her lying as still as death, her face pale and a circle of blood staining her shoulder.

Ken lay facedown, not moving, a few feet from Jennie.

Resisting the urge to put a bullet through the man's head, Cameron hurried toward Jennie.

"Jennie?" Cameron dropped to his knees beside her and pushed her hair from her face. "Jennie?"

She didn't move or respond to his call. All his memories of this woman played through his mind like a video recording, recreating all the good times they'd had together when they were young and the way she made him feel now. She couldn't be gone. He pressed his fingers to her throat feeling for a pulse. After several long seconds, he felt the steady beat of blood beneath the skin. She was alive. As his family gathered behind, Cameron pressed a kiss to Jennie's forehead. "Wake up, sweetheart."

"Cameron! Watch out!" Logan cried out.

Cameron looked up in time to see Ken lunge toward the pistol. He grabbed the gun and rolled to his feet.

No! Cameron couldn't allow him to hurt Jennie or any of his family. The closest man to Ken, Cameron leaped to his feet and charged after him.

In a champion football tackle his high school coach would have been proud of, Cameron dived for Ken's legs. But the man had the gun pointed to his own head and pulled the trigger before Cameron's body clipped him and sent him sprawling across the ground.

For the last time, gunfire echoed off the sheer rock face of the bluffs. Then Ken lay against the ground, his breathing coming in gasps, the side of his head a bloody mess. But he was still conscious. Barely.

When Cameron turned back to Jennie, she was pushing to a sitting position, using her uninjured arm. "You okay?"

"Yeah, don't worry about me."

Don't worry about her? Was she kidding? He'd been knotted up inside since he'd first heard she was in danger. Don't worry about her. He squatted next to her and pushed her shirt aside to see the injured shoulder. "Hurt bad?" The bullet had nicked the fleshy part of her shoulder, but hadn't gone in.

She pulled her collar back up. "See? It's just a flesh wound." With a jerk of her chin, she shot a look at Ken. "Deal with him."

Jack had caught up with the rest of them and knelt down next to Ken. "He's lost a lot of blood."

"Ask him who's behind this," Cameron called out.

"You're dying, buddy, and confession is good for the soul. Who's behind all this?" Jack asked.

Ken's eyes closed, and for a moment, Cameron thought the man had slipped away. Then his eyelids rose halfway. "Made a bad investment."

"We know. With Kingston Trust." Jack removed his shirt and wadded it up to press against the man's head.

After a long pause, Ken whispered, "It didn't stop there. Kingston is only the front. I didn't know it was a lifetime investment." He laughed, the sound coming out as a cough. "The boss sent me in to secure this deal. Said if I didn't get the Wards off their land, I shouldn't bother returning to Denver."

Cameron left Jennie with his mother and joined Jack. "Did Kingston Trust send you because of the oil?" He hoped that Ken would hold on long enough to give them all the information he needed.

"Yeah." His head rolled to the side as if too heavy to hold up. "Only not just Kingston."

"Who's the boss?" Cameron demanded.

Ken's eyes widened briefly. "Can't say."

"Who's the other investor you know about?"

He mumbled something unintelligible, his voice fading into the air.

"Who, damn it!" They needed to know who was next on the list. This man couldn't die until they did. Cameron resisted the urge to reach out to lift the man by the collar and shake him.

The color in his face faded into a deathly pale gray and his lids closed. "Figure it out for yourself." The last word came out in a light rush of the man's dying breath. His face went slack, a peaceful expression relaxing the pained frown on his forehead.

Jack removed the shirt he'd pressed against the man's head and sat back on his haunches.

Ken Bennett was gone.

JENNIE HAD NEVER FELT so tired. She could stand and she could move, except for raising her injured arm. But now that the danger was over, she felt as limp, unco-ordinated and weak as a day-old colt.

When she swayed on her feet, Cameron scooped her into his arms. "Let's go home."

"To the Flying W?" Jennie leaned into his arms, enjoying the way he made her feel warm all over and protected. She could get used to having her own personal bodyguard, if the bodyguard was always Cameron.

Tom Morgan stepped in front of Cameron, blocking his path. "No. Home to the Bar M."

Jennie frowned. "What do you mean?"

Tom glanced at his wife and back to Jennie. "I mean I've been a fool for long enough. I owe you and your father an apology."

Jennie didn't know how to respond to such a declaration and she leaned against Cameron, hoping for inspiration.

But Tom wasn't done. "And I owe an apology to you, Cameron, for trying to live your life for you. So, you're not a rancher. You're good at what you do with Prescott Personal Securities. I see that now."

Cameron stared over the top of Jennie's head at his father. "Apology accepted."

"Soon as your father gets home from the hospital, I'd like to come over and have a talk with him." Tom smiled. "Think you could lock his gun cabinet long enough for me to get in?"

Jennie laughed, hope filling her chest with warmth no amount of sunshine could ever produce. "I think I can manage." The thirty-year-old feud was almost over.

Although she could have walked, she liked having Cameron carry her. But with his family looking on, she felt shy and conspicuous. "Uh, you can let me go now, Cameron."

"Never again, Jennie."

Chapter Eighteen

"What do you mean Tom Morgan's coming to my house. I'll believe it when I see pigs fly." Hank Ward sat with his foot propped up in his lounge chair, his face flushed a bright shade of red, cranky as ever from his stay in the hospital.

Jennie stood in front of him, her arms crossed over her chest. "Mr. Morgan's coming and you *will* be nice."

Cameron stood by the door, a smile playing around the corners of his mouth. He loved it when Jennie was mad. Her eyes flashed a harvest-wheat gold and she flicked her hair over her shoulders, like a horse irritated by a pesky fly. Yeah, his Jennie was a woman to contend with. And she was his Jennie. Just as soon as he told her she was.

"Tom Morgan's coming over to bury the hatchet and end this feud once and for all."

Cameron winced at her wording.

"More than likely he'll bury the hatchet in my head," Hank muttered.

"Daaaddd." Jennie tapped her booted toe on the wood flooring.

"Okay. I'll try to be nice." He glanced at Cameron. "For Cameron's sake, I'll try to be nice."

Jennie stepped back, her eyes going wide. "That's a change."

As he shifted in his chair, Hank grimaced and looked anywhere but at Cameron or Jennie. "I had some time to think while I was incarcerated in that dadblamed hospital."

His daughter's head tipped to the side and she asked softly, "Come to any conclusions?"

"Yeah, I was wrong about your bodyguard. He did a good job and kept you safe. Can't fault him with that." Hank grabbed Jennie's hand. "Jennie, Cameron?" He held out his other hand. "I guess if I can trust you with my daughter's life, I can trust you with just about anything."

Cameron moved forward and took the extended hand in a firm grip. "Thank you, sir."

He glared at Ms. Blainey. "Rachel, will you leave us for a moment? I have something I want to say and I can't say it in front of you."

Ms. Blainey harrumphed and turned away. "Guess I have something to do in the kitchen."

When she'd left the room, Hank waved Jennie and Cameron closer. "Like I said, I trust you, Cameron, and I know if I can trust you with my daughter, I can trust you with a secret."

Hank had him curious now. What could Hank know that was so important he had to send the housekeeper out of the room to tell him?

Then he hit him with it. "Two years ago when Robert Prescott's plane went down, he didn't die in the crash." After he dropped the bomb, he sat back in his chair and waited for Cameron's response.

"Evangeline's Robert? Head of Prescott Personal Se-curities?" Cameron had a hard time grasping the concept. After thinking the man had died in an airplane crash, he wasn't prepared to learn something completely opposite. "How do you know this? Hell, how do you know him?"

"Bob and I go way back to Vietnam. He was working an undercover operation to ferret out Americans selling weapons to the Viet Cong. I had the inside on it and he collected the information to nail the guys." Hank shrugged as if the incident meant little. "We kept in touch. And when he came through here a couple months back, I found him a place to stay."

"The hunting cabin up in the aspen ridge area of the ranch?" Jennie asked.

Her father nodded. "Yup."

"I thought you were getting it ready for the hunting season awful early." Jennie shook her head. "So that's what you were up to."

"Had to help out an old friend and keep it hush-hush."

Cameron paced across the wood floor, his boot heels tapping. "Why didn't you tell Evangeline?"

"He made me promise to keep it a secret. As long as he was 'dead' Evangeline and his family were safe, from what I don't know."

Stopping in front of Hank's chair, Cameron pushed a hand through his hair. "Wow. She'll be ecstatic when she finds out."

Hank put out a hand and clasped Cameron's arm. "You can't tell anyone else. I promised."

"Even Evangeline?"

Hank shook his head. "Not even her. He made me promise."

Cameron stood straight and let out a long breath. How could he keep such a secret from the man's wife?

She'd been heartbroken when she'd learned of her husband's death. Evangeline had done so much for Cameron he felt he owed her the truth.

As if reading his thoughts, Hank repeated. "You can't tell her. Do I have your word?"

Without hesitation, Cameron answered. "Yes, sir." If Hank trusted him with this big a secret, he could trust him to keep it. "Where is Mr. Prescott now?"

"If I knew, I probably wouldn't be at liberty to tell you. However, I don't know. Rachel!" Hank shouted. "Where's that lemonade you promised me?"

"You sure you should be shouting so much?" Jennie fluffed the pillow beneath Hank's injured ankle.

The older man tapped a hand to his chest. "Keeps my lungs healthy. Doctor said so."

"Good, cause I don't know what I'd do without you around here yelling at me." She smiled to soften her words.

When she straightened, Hank grabbed her wrist. "Don't know what I'd do if I were to lose you, Jennie. You remind me so much of your mother."

"Hank." Ms. Blainey carried the usual tray of lemonade into the living room, a stern look on her normally pleasant face. "Don't you have something to say to your daughter?"

Jennie's brows dipped downward.

"I was getting to that." He cleared his throat. "Now that the government is going to come in and harvest the oil on our land, I can afford to hire more hands. Jennie, you don't have to stay if you don't want to. In fact, I insist you get out and get your own life."

Jennie's face paled and she shot a glance toward Cameron.

The way Hank made it sound, he was kicking Jennie out of the house. What the heck? Did she think her father would kick her out of the only home she knew and loved? Hank would die before he did that.

Cameron hadn't had two minutes alone with Jennie since the police had come to collect Doug's and Ken's bodies the previous afternoon. The bullet found in Vance Franklin's skull matched Ken's pistol, thus clearing Jennie though she had more reason than anyone to kill her husband.

From Jennie's account, Doug Sweeney had been working on his own to drive the Wards from their land. The only connection between him and Ken Bennett was that they were directed by the same boss. Doug clearly hadn't wanted to kill anyone. For his loyalty, he'd taken a bullet and died.

Between filling out reports until dark and his family monopolizing their time like one big, happy family reunion, he hadn't gotten Jennie alone to tell her how he felt and what they should do about it.

This morning had been tied up with the drive to the hospital in Denver to bring her father home, and now his family was due to arrive any minute, eager to mend the rift and get on with a neighborly life. All tasks needed to be done, but it all meant he wouldn't have Jennie alone now for hours.

While Hank went on with his reasoning for pushing Jennie out of the house, Cameron turned and slipped through the screen door onto the deck. His booted feet paced the full length of the deck stretching across the front of the house. When he turned to walk back, Jennie stood in his path, her forehead creased in a frown.

"Jennie, we need to talk," he blurted. No finesse, no

warning, just an incredibly intense need to get their lives straight.

She inhaled a deep breath and let it out slowly. "You're ready to leave, aren't you?" Her gold eyes shone with unshed tears. "It's okay. I understand. You wouldn't be happy out here and I wouldn't be happy anywhere else, right?"

When he opened his mouth to contradict her statement, she held up her hand. "No, let me finish."

Tense, but curious as to where she was going, he leaned against a post and crossed his arms over his chest. "I'm listening."

"Ten years ago, you asked me if I'd leave the Flying W and go with you wherever you landed." She pushed her long, blond hair behind her ears. "Back then, I was young and afraid of losing my father. Now, I'm not so young and still afraid of losing my father."

Cameron's stomach clenched and he pushed away from the post. This was it, the point of no return. The time Jennie would once and for all tell him to leave without her, that their love could never be strong enough to endure. His teeth ground together and the muscles in his jaw twitched. This time he wouldn't let her go without a fight.

Jennie continued before he could open his mouth. "I'm afraid of a lot of things, but I'm more afraid of losing the only man I ever loved." She looked up at him, tears slipping down her cheeks. "Cameron, I know it's been a long time, but is that offer still open? Will you still let me come with you wherever you land?"

Cameron's ears rang so loud, he didn't hear her last words. All he heard was "the man she loved." He assumed she meant her father. If he didn't at least fight for her and make her see he was the right man for her, he'd kick himself for the rest of his life. "I don't care what your father told you. You belong here on the ranch, but you also belong to me. I'm not leaving this time unless you go with me. Do you hear that, Jennie Ward?" Cameron grasped her shoulders and shook her gently. "I've always loved you and regretted leaving you the minute I stepped off the Flying W. If you don't come with me, I'll stay right here and drive your father nuts, do you hear me? Nuts!"

"Cameron?"

He inhaled, ready to launch into his next diatribe, putting more words together than he'd ever wanted, knowing if he didn't convince her, he'd regret it for the rest of his life.

"Cameron?"

"What?" His question was more of shout.

"Didn't you hear what I said? I love you and want to go with you no matter where."

"Damn right you will." Then her words sank in and he stood stock-still letting the full meaning make it all the way to his brain. When it did, his world rocked.

Jennie Ward loved him and wanted to go with him. "But I want to stay here. You don't have to go anywhere. We can be happy right here."

"What about your job?"

"I can commute." Cameron pulled her into his arms.

Her fingers circled behind his neck and laced into the hair at his nape. "You can?"

"I'll be gone a lot." He brushed the hair behind her ears, thinking about how he could brush her hair for her a lot more if they were together.

"But you'll come home to me, right?" Jennie rose on her tiptoes and pressed a kiss to his chin.

"Yes, to you." He kissed her scarred eyebrow. "*And* the ranch." He dropped a kiss on her other eyebrow. "*And* our big, stubborn, ornery families." He kissed the tip of her nose.

Out of the corner of his eye, he noted that a truck had pulled into the drive and was unloading. Why now? He wasn't done.

"Are you talking about the Morgans?" Logan was first to butt in. Figured. "Does this mean you're sticking around?"

Cameron didn't glance at his brother, his gaze was locked with Jennie's. "Looks that way."

"Good," Logan said. Then he turned to his father. "Dad, if it's all the same to you, now that we have the financial support we need to hire hands for the ranch, I'm moving to Denver to go back to school."

Tom's face flushed a bright red. "Since when did you think you needed to go to school?"

"Since before Cameron left. I've always wanted to go to college, but with Cameron gone, didn't feel like I could leave it all to you." For the first time in a long time, Logan smiled a real smile free of the usual scowl. "I guess I was a bit disappointed."

"A bit?" Emma Morgan rolled her eyes. "You've been a growly bear for almost ten years. Please, go!"

Logan's grin widened. "I think I can get enrolled by this fall and maybe Molly and I can room together. How about it, Molly?"

"Forget it." Molly climbed the porch stairs. "I don't want some smelly brother messing up my dating life. Get your own place."

Logan looped an arm around her middle and rubbed his knuckles in her hair. "Admit it, you'd love to have a male chaperone to keep you safe, wouldn't you?"

Wanting Jennie to himself, Cameron cleared his throat. "Do you all mind, I have business to discuss with Jennie."

"Yeah. Business." Logan snorted, but he climbed the steps and entered through the door Jennie held open for him.

Jennie shouted inside, "Dad, you have company." To Cameron's family, she smiled and held the door. "Just go on in, my father's expecting you."

"He's not armed is he?" Tom asked.

Emma hit him in the gut and shoved him through the door.

When the last Morgan cleared the door and disappeared inside, Jennie melted into Cameron's arms.

Finally, he had her where he wanted her and this time he wasn't letting go. His lips descended in a soul-defining kiss, sealing their pact to be together forever.

Epilogue

Evangeline sat with her legs neatly crossed, staring at the photograph on her desk. The sun shone over Denver and summer would soon be here. Change was in the air, but some things never changed.

She stared at Robert's smiling blue eyes.

How she wished he were by her side. Prescott Personal Securities had been his dream, but sometimes, keeping his dream alive was hard, requiring a lot of strength. Strength she sometimes wondered if she had.

A light knock on the open door drew her attention to the woman standing there.

With one last glance at her beloved husband, Evangeline drew in a deep breath and stood. "Come in, Sara, and have a seat."

At five feet four inches with beautiful brown wavy hair hanging loose around her shoulders and light green eyes, Sara Montgomery didn't look mean enough to be a bodyguard.

From a wealthy background, she'd been born with the proverbial silver spoon in her mouth, wanting for nothing. When she'd come of age, she'd turned her back on the very life she'd been born to and went into a career in law enforcement.

"Mrs. Prescott." Sara sank onto the leather seat and crossed her legs like any other debutante.

Evangeline resisted the smile twitching the edges of her lips. The more she perused Sara, the more she realized she'd made the right decision. She lifted the file on her desk and thumbed through the pages.

"Sara, during your time in the FBI, did you conduct undercover operations?"

"Yes, ma'am, on numerous occasions."

"Did you have any difficulties assuming different identities?"

Sara shook her head. "None, whatsoever. I played the role of a hooker, a corporate executive, a high school teenager and an old woman, to name a few."

Evangeline nodded and flipped a few more pages and stopped on her family background. "I understand you hail from a long line of debutantes."

"Yes, ma'am, but I left that behind when I left home at eighteen. It in no way shapes the way I do my job. I was trained in hand-to-hand combat and an entire arsenal of weaponry in the FBI. I can do most anything any man can do, only better."

"I have no doubt about that. However, what I need you to do is infiltrate a corporation by the name of Tri Corp. Media. To do it might require you to act in a role you might find repugnant."

"Ma'am, I can do anything. I like my work with Prescott Personal Securities. You can assign me to anything. I'll do it. Just name it."

"As you know TCM is directly connected to Kingston Investment Group through the purchase of land secured from Investors in Kingston Trust."

"Yes, ma'am, I've been briefed."

"I need you to get inside and find out who's really in charge and what exactly they're up to."

"Do you want me to go in as a new-hire or corporate executive?"

"No, I want you to go in as a debutante." Evangeline gave the news a minute to sink in.

For a long moment, Sara sat motionless, all emotions hidden behind a smooth, sophisticated and bland expression. The only indication of the effect her request had on Sara was the small twitch in the skin beneath her right eye.

Evangeline broke the silence with, "Are you up to the challenge?"

Sara inhaled a long steady breath and blew it out slowly, her shoulders squaring. "Yes, ma'am. When do I start?"

* * * * *

BODYGUARDS UNLIMITED, DENVER, COLORADO, *continues next month.*
Sara Montgomery infiltrates the world she happily left behind in Kathleen Long's HIGH SOCIETY SABOTAGE.
Look for it only in Harlequin Intrigue!

MEDITERRANEAN NIGHTS

Join the guests and crew of **Alexandra's Dream,**
*the newest luxury ship to set sail on the
romantic Mediterranean, as they experience
the glamorous world of cruising.*

*A new Harlequin continuity series
begins in June 2007 with*
FROM RUSSIA, WITH LOVE
by Ingrid Weaver

*Marina Artamova books a cabin on the luxurious
cruise ship* **Alexandra's Dream,** *when she finds
out that her orphaned nephew and his
adoptive father are aboard. She's determined
to be reunited with the boy…but the romantic
ambience of the ship and her undeniable
attraction to a man she considers her enemy
are about to interfere with her quest!*

Turn the page for a sneak preview!

Piraeus, Greece

"THERE SHE IS, Stefan. *Alexandra's Dream.*" David Anderson squatted beside his new son and pointed at the dark blue hull that towered above the pier. The cruise ship was a majestic sight, twelve decks high and as long as a city block. A circle of silver and gold stars, the logo of the Liberty Cruise Line, gleamed from the swept-back smokestack. Like some legendary sea creature born for the water, the ship emanated power from every sleek curve—even at rest it held the promise of motion. "That's going to be our home for the next ten days."

The child beside him remained silent, his cheeks working in and out as he sucked furiously on his thumb. Hair so blond it appeared white ruffled against his forehead in the harbor breeze. The baby-sweet scent unique to the very young mingled with the tang of the sea.

"Ship," David said. "Uh, *parakhod.*"

From beneath his bangs, Stefan looked at the *Alexandra's Dream.* Although he didn't release his thumb, the corners of his mouth tightened with the beginning of a smile.

David grinned. That was Stefan's first smile this afternoon, one of only two since they had left the orphanage yesterday. It was probably because of the boat—according to the orphanage staff, the boy loved boats, which was the main reason David had decided to book this cruise. Then again, there was a strong possibility the smile could have been a reaction to David's attempt at pocket-dictionary Russian. Whatever the cause, it was a good start.

The liaison from the adoption agency had claimed that Stefan had been taught some English, but David had yet to see evidence of it. David continued to speak, positive his son would understand his tone even if he couldn't grasp the words. "This is her maiden voyage. Her first trip, just like this is our first trip, and that makes it special." He motioned toward the stage that had been set up on the pier beneath the ship's bow. "That's why everyone's celebrating."

The ship's official christening ceremony had been held the day before and had been a closed affair, with only the cruise-line executives and VIP guests invited, but the stage hadn't yet been disassembled. Banners bearing the blue and white of the Greek flag of the ship's owner, as well as the Liberty circle-of-stars logo, draped the edges of the platform. In the center, a group of musicians and a dance troupe dressed in traditional white folk costumes performed for the benefit of the *Alexandra's Dream*'s first passengers. Their audience was in a festive mood, snapping their fingers in time to the music while the dancers twirled and wove through their steps.

David bobbed his head to the rhythm of the mandolins. They were playing a folk tune that seemed vaguely familiar, possibly from a movie he'd seen. He hummed a few notes. "Catchy melody, isn't it?"

Stefan turned his gaze on David. His eyes were a striking shade of blue, as cool and pale as a winter horizon and far too solemn for a child not yet five. Still, the smile that hovered at the corners of his mouth persisted. He moved his head with the music, mirroring David's motion.

David gave a silent cheer at the interaction. Hopefully, this cruise would provide countless opportunities for more. "Hey, good for you," he said. "Do you like the music?"

The child's eyes sparked. He withdrew his thumb with a pop. *"Moozika!"*

"Music. Right!" David held out his hand. "Come on, let's go closer so we can watch the dancers."

Stefan grasped David's hand quickly, as if he feared it would be withdrawn. In an instant his budding smile was replaced by a look close to panic.

Did he remember the car accident that had killed his parents? It would be a mercy if he didn't. As far as David knew, Stefan had never spoken of it to anyone. Whatever he had seen had made him run so far from the crash that the police hadn't found him until the next day. The event had traumatized him to the extent that he hadn't uttered a word until his fifth week at the orphanage. Even now he seldom talked.

David sat back on his heels and brushed the hair from Stefan's forehead. That solemn, too-old gaze locked with his, and for an instant, David felt as if he looked back in time at an image of himself thirty years ago.

He didn't need to speak the same language to understand exactly how this boy felt. He knew what it meant to be alone and powerless among strangers, trying to be brave and tough but wishing with every fiber of his being for a place to belong, to be safe, and most of all for someone to love him....

He knew in his heart he would be a good parent to Stefan. It was why he had never considered halting the adoption process after Ellie had left him. He hadn't balked when he'd learned of the recent claim by Stefan's spinster aunt, either; the absentee relative had shown up too late for her case to be considered. The adoption was meant to be. He and this child already shared a bond that went deeper than paperwork or legalities.

A seagull screeched overhead, making Stefan start and press closer to David.

"That's my boy," David murmured. He swallowed hard, struck by the simple truth of what he had just said.

That's my *boy*.

"I CAN'T BE PATIENT, RUDOLPH. I'm not going to stand by and watch my nephew get ripped from his country and his roots to live on the other side of the world."

Rudolph hissed out a slow breath. "Marina, I don't like the sound of that. What are you planning?"

"I'm going to talk some sense into this American kidnapper."

"No. Absolutely not. No offence, but diplomacy is not your strong suit."

"Diplomacy be damned. Their ship's due to sail at five o'clock."

"Then you wouldn't have an opportunity to speak with him even if his lawyer agreed to a meeting."

"I'll have ten days of opportunities, Rudolph, since I plan to be on board that ship."

* * * * *

Follow Marina and David as they join forces to uncover the reason behind little Stefan's unusual silence, and the secret behind the death of his parents....

Look for FROM RUSSIA, WITH LOVE by Ingrid Weaver in stores June 2007.

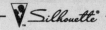

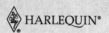
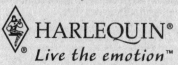

REQUEST YOUR FREE BOOKS!

2 FREE NOVELS PLUS 2 FREE GIFTS!

HARLEQUIN®
INTRIGUE®

Breathtaking Romantic Suspense

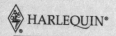

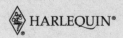

HARLEQUIN®

INTRIGUE®

COMING NEXT MONTH

#993 HIGH SOCIETY SABOTAGE by Kathleen Long
Bodyguards Unlimited, Denver, CO (Book 4 of 6)
In order to blend into the world of CEO Stephen Turner, PPS agent Sara Montgomery adopts the role she left behind years ago—debutante—to stop investors from dying.

#994 ROYAL LOCKDOWN by Rebecca York
Lights Out (Book 1 of 4)
A brand-new continuity! Princess Ariana LeBron brought the famous Beau Pays sapphire to Boston, which security expert Shane Peters intended to steal. But plans changed when an act of revenge plunged Boston into a complete blackout.

#995 COLBY VS. COLBY by Debra Webb
Colby Agency: The Equalizers (Book 3 of 3)
Does the beginning of the Equalizers mean the end of the Colby Agency? Jim Colby and Victoria Camp-Colby go head-to-head when they both send agents to L.A., where nothing is as simple as it seems.

#996 SECRET OF DEADMAN'S COULEE by B.J. Daniels
Whitehorse, Montana
A downed plane in Missouri Breaks badlands was bad enough. But on board was someone who was murdered thirty-two years ago? Sheriff Carter Jackson and Eve Bailey thought their reunion would be hard enough....

#997 SHOWDOWN WITH THE SHERIFF by Jan Hambright
Sheriff Logan Brewer called Rory Matson back to Reaper's Point, not to identify her father's body, but the skull discovered in his backpack at the time of his death.

#998 FORBIDDEN TEMPTATION by Paula Graves
Women were dying in Birmingham's trendy nightclub district, and only Rose Browning saw a killer's pattern emerging. But she didn't know how to stop him, not until hot-shot criminal profiler Daniel Hartman arrived.